WITH ARMS
WIDE OPEN

COMPILED BY

VANILLA HEART PUBLISHING

VANILLA HEART PUBLISHING
USA

WITH ARMS WIDE OPEN
Copyright 2009 Vanilla Heart Publishing

Published by: Vanilla Heart Publishing
www.vanillaheartbooksandauthors.com
10121 Evergreen Way, 25-156
Everett, WA 98204 USA

ISBN: 978-1-935407-20-1
LCCN: 2009924106

10 9 8 7 6 5 4 3 2 1 First Edition

First Printing, March 2009
Printed in the United States of America

WELCOME

Vanilla Heart Publishing is proud to present *With Arms Wide Open* — an amazing collection of heartwarming and inspirational stories and poems from a group of talented authors sharing their stories of living life *with arms wide open.*

Kimberlee Williams
Managing Editor
Vanilla Heart Publishing
http://www.vanillaheartbooksandauthors.com

TABLE OF CONTENTS

AUTHOR INFORMATION
WWW.VANILLAHEARTBOOKSANDAUTHORS.COM

THE VISIT

LILLITH T. LEWIS

When my mother was diagnosed with cancer, I lived 3,000 miles away, and my worry constantly nagged like a toothache. I'd call my parents, but they spoke in platitudes. My uncle-the-doctor claimed my mother was getting the best medical treatment available — a clichéd phrase that meant nothing to me and offered little comfort.

I offered to fly back to help. "No," Dad said, "You've got a child. We'll handle things." Caught between relief and concern, I decided that her illness must not be too bad if he didn't want me to come.

However, a short time later, the doctors performed surgery and Mom had what the medical profession euphemistically called a setback. My telephone calls to my parents became more insistent: I wanted to be with them. Dad responded, "Your mother doesn't want you to see her like this."

Such sad proof of how formal our relationship had become. Yes, my mother had always been slightly vain about her looks, but how could she refuse a visit by her only daughter for such a silly reason. No matter how often I called, my father repeated that Mom didn't want me to see her looking this way. He maintained that my mother would return to health and then I could visit. Perhaps in this way they could pretend things would get better, but I needed to know if she really would recover.

With determination, I called my uncle-the-doctor. Because I refused to let him sidestep my pointed questions, he confirmed the seriousness of my mother's health. Things weren't good and they were unlikely to get better. He ended the conversation with the words, "You should fly home soon." Although it was unspoken, I hung up knowing that my mother had little time left.

Fine, if my parents refused to give me permission to visit, I wouldn't ask; I would just do it. My husband agreed to my idea. I very quickly had airplane tickets for myself, and our little son. Then I called my Dad and told him when we would arrive. After he said, "Now, now, that's not such a good idea," I replied, "If you won't pick us up at the airport, I'll call the other relatives and see if one of them will." Nope, I wasn't above a tad bit of blackmail. Sighing, he put the telephone down and talked to my mother. When he finally returned, he said he would be glad to pick us up at the airport.

During the entire eight-hour trip, and despite the task of inventing activities to occupy a child, I kept my determination to handle whatever happened. I would return as a self-assured adult. My certainty remained with me right up to the minute I walked into my mother's bedroom. Whatever I had expected, this excruciatingly gaunt person stunned me. Once she noticed me, I responded to my mother's greetings by rote. Guilty for feeling relieved at the distraction, I allowed my son to pull me out of the room.

"Mommy, where's Grandma? Let's find Grandma." So changed was my mother that my child didn't recognize his grandmother and wanted me to help him search for her.

"Honey, that is Grandma; she's been sick."

"That's not Grandma! Grandma doesn't look like that!"

There's nothing like a small child to bring things out into the open. Certainly the individual lying on the bed was shocking to see. Since the last time I had seen her, less than a year ago, she had aged forty years. In fact, she looked like the World War II photographs of the people who had been released from concentration camps.

Eventually I sidetracked my son by depositing his toys on the living room floor (something I never would have tried if my mother had been well), and I wandered off to see what I could find to make for dinner.

Some time later, I found myself staring out of the kitchen window at the peach tree in the backyard. Forgetting the onions I had been chopping, leaving food and pans scattered across the counter, I desperately denied the existence of yellowed skin pulled tight across the emaciated body. I wanted to ignore the memory of bony hands, straw-like hair and haunted eyes.

With the murmuring of my parents' voices in the background, I wondered what I was doing there. I had no idea how to handle this situation. Nothing had prepared me for this.

My dad entered the kitchen. "Your mother wanted me to tell you that she's glad you're here."

There it was, out in the open. Once again, Dad was running interference between his wife and his daughter. Truthfully, my mother and I hadn't openly and honestly communicated in years. Sure, I called her regularly, but our calls followed a consistent script, something like this: My father would answer the phone and after a brief period of dialogue, he would say, "Your mother wants to talk to you." Then I'd hear him walk into the other room and tell my mother that I was on the phone. She'd speak into the telephone tenuously, as if she wasn't sure it would really be my voice she'd hear. I'd pretend everything was wonderful between us.

"Hi Mom, how are you doing?"

"How are you? What's that husband of yours doing?"

"I'm good, Mom. We're doing fine. He likes his new job a lot."

"How is my grandson?"

"He's great, Mom," and I would enumerate my son's latest accomplishments. She'd respond with grandmotherly comments and soon the call would end.

I loved my mother and I knew she loved me. Yet the distance between us had solidified over time. Whenever we talked, I expected a judgment or misunderstanding. For that reason, we always stuck to safe topics.

When my father repeated that my mother was glad I had come, I realized that I had been standing in silence for too long. Suddenly I saw his exhaustion. His skin was dull, and his eyes were rimmed with grey. He, too, had grown older from my mother's illness.

Instinctively I reached out to hug him. "Oh, Dad, I'll do whatever I can while I'm here."

And so we began. My father taught me how to take care of Mom, explained about her medicines and what to do if she stopped breathing. Together, the two of us worked to give her what comfort we could.

The next day, in place of the nurse, I stayed with Mom while Dad and my son visited relatives. While they were gone, Mom choked once. I did what Dad had said to do. Wonderfully, incredibly, it worked! She started breathing again.

Afterwards we both pretended that nothing had happened. Acting with a calmness that I certainly didn't feel, we settled back to watch a talk show together.

Throughout the afternoon, we commented erratically about the guests on the TV shows and about her grandson and other relatives. Unimportant remarks filled the conversation. As Mom drifted in and out of sleep, I chased my emotions. My thoughts bounced around like water surging over rocks after the rupture of a dam.

Books I had read mentioned that I should talk about the problems of the past so that we could forgive each other. First, I decided to start a conversation about happy times when we were comfortable in each other's company. Then I would work around to talking about serious topics. Tentatively, I mentioned how much fun it had been playing cards together after school. She interrupted my reminiscing. "When your dad and I first married, I used to play bridge, but I stopped. It was so hard to find good bridge partners."

Her words hit me like a blow to the gut. My mother didn't remember the nonstop games of blackjack, hearts, gin rummy, and pinochle. For years, we played together. Laughing, joking, asking advice about boys, discussing politics — while we played cards we talked about almost any topic and yet never forgot the score. Often my neighborhood friends had joined our daily games as a third in pinochle.

All of her life, until now, my mother could retain information about a dress someone had worn to dinner long ago. Perhaps the strategy for reconciliation might have worked then. But the woman my mother had become didn't remember those painful incidents that still stung in my mind years later. And she certainly didn't remember the stilted formality that had passed for our relationship more recently. With that realization came another one. The last thing I wanted to do was to dredge up old arguments and hurtful events that she wouldn't even remember. To me, that would be mean and spiteful. Besides, she was dying. It seemed silly to analyze our past relationship.

I soon realized her personality was oddly muted. Gone was the wit that used to pop out at random moments. What could I do while she slowly faded away? I had no power to stop this insidious disease that had invaded our lives. Perhaps I could not ask my frail mother to forgive me — and maybe it didn't really matter since she couldn't remember the things that needed forgiveness. No, I couldn't change the past, but I could forgive her.

I thought of the stories told at family reunions about my mother walking the floor with the baby who wouldn't stop crying. I was that baby. Surely she felt frustration then but she didn't give up. I couldn't give up on her now. I knew in my heart and my head that this would be my last visit with her.

As the talk show host blathered to a silly young starlet, something in my attitude changed. This individual wasn't just any sick person. I couldn't keep pretending that I was taking care of someone else's mother. Regardless of our past differences, she deserved my compassion simply because she was my mother. And I did love her. In spite of her illness — or because of it — she deserved better in her final days. Maybe we would rediscover the warmth that had been between us years ago. In any case, I needed to rediscover what we had lost over the years. She might not understand what had changed and she might not notice any difference in my behavior, but I would swallow my pride and my anger. Regardless of her behavior, I would treat her kindly and honestly.

Working up my nerve during the next commercial, I said, "Mom, when you stopped breathing, I was so scared. Does that happen often?" When she didn't respond, I continued, "I'm glad it worked. I don't know what I would have done if it hadn't. Does it didn't hurt you?"

Stopping often to swallow, slowly she answered. "You did fine. The nurse that comes three times a week is pretty good. She's careful and helps me. The other one is okay, but sometimes she . . ."

With the release of nervousness that followed my statement, I missed much of what she said. As I reached for her hand, I realized that I had made a start.

At some point in the afternoon, I moved to sit next to her on the bed. When my father came home from work, I was still sitting there. I could tell he was pleased. Later that night, he mentioned that she hadn't let anyone else sit on the bed with her.

In this way, we continued. On the days Dad worked, I stayed with Mom. What a change of pace for me! I was used to busy days with my family and job. Now life slowed down as I settled into the roles of caregiver and housewife.

Every day I cooked meals, played with my son, and sat with my mother. However, most of my time was spent cooking. Knowing that people with cancer have little appetite, I carried in a tray of food into Mom every few hours. When she enjoyed the beef stroganoff, I was thrilled that she asked for a second helping. Thinking it might help her gain back some weight I created other rich dishes. When she had difficulty swallowing, I tempted her with homemade milk shakes or fruit and yogurt smoothies. Without doubt, my son was willing to test the experimental drinks.

Still, I mulled over past incidents. And so, while both my son and my mother napped, I cleaned the house and then meditated. To keep my wits, I needed the calmness meditation produced. Constantly, I listened for two voices: my child's and my mother's. Before dinner, Dad would come home and I would update him on the day's events. After dinner, I would take my child for a walk. Oh, how I needed to experience the outdoors through his youthful curiosity!

Unhurriedly the days and nights passed. Frequently, I sat with Mom as she watched television. Slowly, as I listened for my mother's breathing (or rather, guarded her from the lack of breathing), guilt, anger and resentment no longer ruled my behavior. I didn't know what would happen and so I set aside my preconceptions. Finally I realized that continuing to react out of pain and anger would change nothing. If I didn't change, Mom would pass over without a chance at understanding and resolution. And I wanted that chance. Expecting the worst at any moment, I no longer searched for perfection in our relationship. When I decided to do what I could for my mother in spite of our past differences, my outlook transformed. I dropped my self-centered agenda. My actions moved away from reacting to her emotions; now I could choose what was right out of love and compassion.

Since her mind had been damaged by the illness and by the many bouts of gasping for air, Mom determined the length and depth of our chats. As the energy behind my emotions depleted, I managed to set aside my long-standing habitual reactions. After that, I was able to openly listen to her complaints and criticism without taking them personally. Actually I could understand them for what they were: the frustrated grievances of a bedridden person in pain. When she wanted to reminisce, rather than judging what she remembered, I enjoyed hearing about it. If she wanted to eat lunch at 10:00 in the morning, I didn't mind because she could always have another later. Even if she didn't notice, it seemed such an easy gift to let her pick the shows we watched. There were so many more important things then quarrelling over the channel!

By focusing on her, I moved outside of myself. My inexperienced attempts at selflessness brought unexpected results. Because I changed my behavior, Mom moved past her typical expectations too. Now when we talked, although our dialogues were not weighty, they were certainly more comfortable.

Finally, for the first time in years, I could remember the good times with my mother. Chopping carrots and potatoes, cooking dinner together, watching as she taught me to make gravy the old-fashioned way. Smiling, I thought of when we argued over the length of my dress. Weekend walks in the woods while fall leaves crunched under our feet. And then I thought back to when I was a proud teenager just learning to drive who chauffeured Mom around town.

All those years ago, were we rehearsing for the roles forces on us by this illness? When she let me take those early steps to adulthood, was I learning the foundation of letting her take the steps she needed in order to handle her physical transition? Certainly we were still learning how to handle our new roles.

All too soon, my son and I had to fly home. What a difference a couple of months had made in my relationship with my parents. Truly, my interactions with Mom had been transformed. Also, I'm sure Dad was relieved that he no longer had to mediate between the two of us.

After we returned home, Dad continually mentioned how "happy your mother and I are that we got to see you." Before long, Mom's voice was too weak to talk on the telephone. Once again, Dad had to relay messages — but this time it wasn't because we were annoyed with each other. He would hold the phone up for Mom to listen as I told her I loved her and missed her. Amazingly, I really meant every word I said.

A few months later, my mother passed.

When her suffering had ended, gratitude accompanied my sorrow. I was so thankful that we had the time to heal our differences. Because of my visit, I could grieve my mother's death without being suffocated by all those years of muddled communications. How much harder it would have been if I had not done it!

STRENGTH AND LOVE AND FAMILY

CHELLE CORDERO

Jenni wasn't easy to come by.

Mark and I decided that we wanted children just a few years into our marriage. We wanted to start our family. But the first two pregnancies "didn't take" – I lost the first at eight weeks and the second at six weeks. Then I got pregnant again. It was an ideal pregnancy, almost no morning sickness and I just felt great.

Jenni was born fourteen days late, a pattern she still continues to this day. When the doctor said "you have a girl", tears came to my eyes as I said, for the very first time, the name that we had picked out for a daughter, Jennifer Rebecca. She is named for my mother, a woman who had passed away just two years before my daughter's birth.

When my beautiful daughter was about a year old I got pregnant again. Something was wrong from the beginning; I was always sick, sick beyond mere morning sickness.

Fortunately, I was a stay-at-home mom, but, as sick as I was, it was still hard to take care of a toddler. Mark worked all day and then came home and took care of the baby because I just didn't have the strength to do it anymore.

About four months into the pregnancy, on a day I just didn't want to get up from bed, Mark and I talked about making the twenty-five minute trip to visit his mom. She was the last remaining parent of our four. He was going to go without me and give me a chance to rest, but instead I decided to go. I am glad that I did because it was the last time I would ever see her.

My mother-in-law complained of exhaustion after visiting her own sick mother in the hospital and she went to lay down for a nap. It wasn't long after when we heard her gasp. She had suffered a massive MI, a heart attack. We tried CPR but it was too late and the responding paramedics pronounced.

I stood up, physically hurting after the compressions of CPR, and I cried. Then the cramping started. The next morning I was rushed to the hospital. The baby I had carried for four months was gone along with our plans and our dreams and the memories of his heartbeat. It wasn't the stress... it was the pregnancy, it wasn't strong. But I got angry at those who tried to tell me that my baby wasn't meant to be. And all I wanted to do was hold my little girl. That is the only thing that kept me going.

After that it was just like my body wasn't "right". The doctor even said it was improbable that I could get pregnant again. Mark and I had really wanted a second child. We wanted a sibling for our daughter. We were discouraged as we looked into adoption and waiting lists and the expense, but at least it was an option.

Then one day after a simple blood test and a check-up, I was told I was pregnant again. And I was terrified. I will admit it now, my biggest fear was not only that I might lose this baby too, but that I would completely lose my mind with it. Then what kind of a mother could I be to my daughter? But we wanted this baby so badly.

By my third month of pregnancy I had an asthma attack and it was quickly followed by another. The doctor told me that asthmatic mothers often miscarry and combined with my previous history, this pregnancy was very high risk. I was medicated for my breathing and put to bed with a two-and-a-half year old child to care for. We had no family in the area and not a lot of money. A neighbor's daughter came over every day after school to take Jenni out to play; the rest of the day was spent in front of the TV. Somehow we managed.

By the end of my second trimester the doctor relaxed his rules for bed rest. One morning at six and a half months I felt restless and edgy. Then late that night I began to hemorrhage. Again I was rushed to the hospital and the next day my son Marc was born by Caesarean section. He was a bouncing baby boy who, even at six-and-a-half weeks early, weighed in at five pounds. Marc Stephen was named for my dad and my mother-in-law. But I developed an infection and I couldn't see my son for the first seven days of his life. We finally got to bring him home in time for his Brit Milah (circumcision), a religious rite of passage.

Last year we got to watch our daughter walk down the aisle to marry the man she loves. Our son is a strapping, tall and handsome young man with a very lovely steady girlfriend. More than two decades have passed since the terror and the tears of lost pregnancies and the joyful births of our children. Mark and I have been blessed with two beautiful children who have grown into adults we are very proud of. We have known the joy of family. Our children have grown into adults and have become our friends. We have been blessed.

I was frantic with worry while I was pregnant with my daughter because of those two earlier misses, but I was terrified while I was pregnant with my son. After losing my four-month pregnancy and burying my mother-in-law within days of each other, I was devastated. It was only with the love and support of my very strong husband and the cuddly arms of my one year old that I survived emotionally. It was that love that brought me through.

BANANA BOATS & BOATLOADS OF COUSINS

K'LEE WILLIAMS

Children don't always have the love and closeness of grandparents and extended families, the dozens of aunties and uncles, hordes of cousins, holiday meals filled with fun and laughter. My childhood family was filled with all these things and more.

My parents decided early on in their marriage that their friends, and our grandparents' friends, would be part of our family, just as much as those born into or adopted into the family. Maybe they really didn't decide at all, it just 'was'. After all, mother's daddy, my Grampy, built his house with an enormous living room, just to accommodate the huge gatherings of friends and family. So, maybe it was just natural, normal, to include everyone in our loving circle.

We children could never call an adult by their first name, oh no! They were 'auntie' this and 'uncle' that. We were all cousins, the many children playing and fighting together, through those years.

We spent most of each summer at Grandma and Grandpa's cabin at the lake. My earliest memories are of a tiny cabin that seemed to grow as I grew. What a wonderful day, the day Grandpa and Dad installed a bathroom inside the cabin, and we no longer had to trudge up the little trail behind the house to the dark and scary outhouse.

The bathtub in the shiny new bathroom inside the cabin was reserved for the grownups, in particular the women. We kids didn't mind that at all, since we spent so much time in the lake anyway. There was always the shower stall on the outside wall of the cabin, built from fiberglass panels for privacy, and a garden hose. That was more bathing than most kids wanted anyway.

Most of the dads would go off to town during the week, and only came 'home' on the weekends. Most of the moms didn't work at outside jobs and spent their summers at the lake. Almost all of the grandma and grandpa generation stayed all through summer, men and women alike, since they were retired.

It was a great childhood.

Grandma would corral a few of the kids to help her make breakfast. Platters mounded with steaming stacks of fluffy pancakes, bowls filled to overflowing with cantaloupe slices, and little jugs of maple syrup. A big yellow pottery jug filled with ice cold milk and coffee for the grownups.

We usually had all our meals out in the covered patio, at three picnic tables laid end to end. Grandma was a bit fussy about things and insisted on tablecloths and manners. That might have seemed incongruous to outsiders, but to all of us it was just, well, just normal. Normal, too, was the happy family, eating their meal in laughter and silliness, elbows knocking into elbows, whether by accident or by purposeful intent, and the inevitable 'hey! He took my pancake!' or 'Mom! She's hogging the syrup!" Subdued is not a word you could ever apply to our family.

After breakfast, some of the kids who hadn't been in on making breakfast and setting the table, did all the clean up, while the lucky ones who had already done their chores of making beds, sweeping out the huge army tent where all the kids slept, or going to fetch water from the natural spring up the road a bit with Grandpa, were free to start their adventures for the day.

We kids wore our bathing suits from dawn to dusk, covered in a big t-shirt only for meals, to abide Grandma's Rule: 'No Hairy Chests at the Table!'

During those long, care-free summers, we built tree forts and camps in the blackberry bushes behind Grampy's house. We hiked 'over the hill' to the small town called Carnation, to Carnation Farms, where we could take the free tour and get a chocolate covered ice cream bar for our attention. We would spend hours and hours tromping through the cedar forest behind the cabin, sometimes not making it back in time for meals, but always having fun, discovering and adventuring, together.

We built pirate ships from old wooden rowboats, with giant bed sheets stolen from Grandma's linen closet for sails, and armed ourselves with cutlasses made of sticks covered with aluminum foil. 'Ahoy, matey,' rang out with the sound of laughter across the lake. Our cannons were squirt guns, our grog - half warm soda pop in the can.

One particularly fun summer, we built a Huckleberry Finn-type raft. Well, we didn't actually build it. A bunch of us cousins decided that we didn't need to build a raft. Our bright idea was to simply unhook the twenty foot long wooden dock Grandpa and the uncles had built and sail that around our own Mighty Mo, Ames Lake.

We gathered up all the oars from all the rowboats lined up against the bulkhead, packed an ice chest full of peanut butter and jelly sandwiches and store brand soda in grape, orange, root beer and cherry, our favorites. My cousin Peter luckily was tall enough to reach the awning attached as s sun shade in front of the cabin, and the grownups were all talking in the back patio and didn't see our handiwork.

Peter and I, as the oldest cousins, herded the twelve or so younger kids onto the dock. Then, we dived under the dock, fumbling with the chains that secured it to the cement filled twenty gallon can anchors underneath the floating dock. The Styrofoam blocks that supported the docks and rafts along the lakeshore were thick and covered in green algae, slippery and home to small fish and interesting floaty things.

Grandpa had a rule, too, although his rule was different from Grandma's rule. His rule was 'Until you can swim down to the Bunker's house and back, you will wear a life preserver whenever you are even near the water.' The Bunker house was about 200 yards down the lake, and Pete and I had passed the Bunker Test years before, in competition with each other, when we were a little more than five years old, almost six years before, to the tune of Grandma and 'the moms' all screaming, "Ernie! Get those babies out of the water! They will drown!" We didn't drown. (We did sleep very soundly that night.)

Peter and I didn't know at the time that Grandpa had already planned for the test and had his friends all along the bank of the lakeshore clear down to Bunker's, ready in case we were having any trouble, to jump in and bring us to shore safely.

We wriggled the kids who hadn't yet passed the Bunker Test into their name-marked life preservers, fastening the straps on the bright orange fluffy pillow-like contraptions. Rick, Wendy, Kris, Tommy, Shelly, Diane, Lee, Johnny, Kaysey, Bill, Andy, and Chip. What a great crew.

We stayed on the lake that day, playing Huck Finn, exploring the coves and backwaters, eating peanut butter and jelly sandwiches washed down with warm cherry sodas, until we heard the dinner bell, ringing faintly across the water from the cabin.

The bell. Whenever the parent type people wanted the kid type people home immediately, one of them would ring the big old ship's bell that hung from the ship's name plate, 'Golden River', and we knew it was time to hotfoot (or paddle fast) back to the cabin, no dawdling! Even now, when I hear a ship's bell, I almost turn around to check to see if grandma is holding dinner or grandpa is making banana boats in the fireplace tucked into the wall of the patio.

You've never had a Banana Boat? Oh my goodness! Banana Boats were a special treat for us kids. Maybe they were so special because it was Grandpa making them for us, pulling the foil wrapped packets from the coals of the dying fire, late at night, after listening to the grownups talk and chatter happily. Could be that, I suppose, but it also might have been the rich, drippy chocolate and warmed bananas, or peeling back the foil carefully exposing the insides of the tasty treat. Or, maybe, it was all of those things.

GRANDPA'S NOT SO VERY SECRET, VERY MESSY, YUMMY BANANA BOAT RECIPE

20 Bananas, ripe not overripe
20 chocolate bars
A roll of foil
A fireplace (preferably outdoors, late at night, while telling stories about the 'old days') Carefully slit the banana peels with a sharp knife. (ADULT JOB)

Carefully slice each banana while still inside the peel into chunks. (ADULT JOB)

KID JOBS:

Hand each kid the following: one banana, one chocolate bar, and a one foot piece of foil.

Have the kids insert a square of chocolate between each chunk of banana, (DON'T BE SURPRISED WHEN CHOCOLATE DISAPPEARS INTO TUMMIES) then wrap the whole banana in foil and twist the ends tight shut. For an added yum factor, sprinkle lightly with cinnamon sugar before wrapping in foil.

Now, the fun part! After ten minutes in the coals, (checking and turning frequently) the banana boats are ready. Pull them out carefully with a pair of fireplace tongs and let them cool a bit before scarfing them right down! Chocolate drips down smiling faces, tummies are full, and you can build a tradition.

After Banana Boats, everyone would settle in for the evening, there in the covered patio, with the fire dying down to an embery glow. Sometimes, we would sing. Sometimes, the grownups would play pinochle. Sometimes, they would tell stories about their own childhoods.

We children would sit there all wrapped cozy in our blankets, our bathing suits drying under our t-shirts 'borrowed' from our daddies, dreaming up our grand adventures for the next day. Sometimes, we would teach each other 'naughty words, like butthead and dorkwad. Or, we would teach each other foreign languages, or go out and lay on our backs on the front yard grass next to the lake, making up new names for the constellations.

And sometimes, my favorite times of all, we would just be together, listening to the frogs sing their mating calls in the shallows of the lake, hearing the odd call of the hoot owl in the big cedar, or the soft laughter of the other families across the lake, distant yet distinct, making their own memories, their own histories.

AT NINE

KATHI ANDERSON

I suppose they're asleep, Mom and Dad. The moon woke me. Or maybe it was the wind. Soundless steps take me to the front door. The heavy wood swings wide at my touch and moonlight pours in, gilding the worn carpet with midnight light.

It had rained, but now stars tickle the sky, bouncing light against a just-past-full moon. The wind has laid, but the grass glints like glass shards, catching and returning the glow from a security lamp in front of the battered brown Ranchero Dad bought last month.

Damp prickling grass raises me to my tiptoes as I head out, the solitary pine tree in my sights. The smells of wet dirt and distant horse manure come to me on a vagrant breeze, mixing with my mother's perfume left in my skin from tonight's tuck-in story and cuddle ritual.

I'm nine now, so we take turns reading to each other, and every night we finish up the bedtime story with raspberries on the cheek, to see who will give in and giggle first. It's usually me.

But now, the tree beckons. Her shadow against the sky entices. I hear the shuffle of stabled horses from that direction, and the plain chant of the tiny stream beneath Cloud 9 bridge. I won't be going that far, but for a moment, I stand in the dark air, seeing in my mind the smooth white round stones of quartz, the crinoids, and the mica flakes we find in the bed of that little trickle. This translucent pebble has a crack in it and I run my thumbnail along its length. That Indian Bead has sand packed in its center, gritty under my fingertips. There. See the bit of mica? It's as big as my little fingernail.

I'm afraid now, in the night. I take a deep breath of cold, filling air. I smell the smell of a night sky. Down the road, Cousin Eugenie's big red cur of a hunting dog barks; three times he barks. The atmosphere around me moves. It's not a breeze but... a shift, and the stars blink out, then return, as the sound of air through feathers gives away an owl in flight.

I'm afraid, here across the fence in the pasture, alone in the night. But the pine tree entices. My fear succumbs to her call.

Feet now accustomed to the wet embrace of grass and weeds, I nearly dance across the remaining yards of early clover. I duck under the drooping branches and get a shower of silver nuggets, baptized by water made holy by its trek through the sky and this tree. Almost giggling with the adrenaline surge of breaking rules and surviving the chill wet of the night, I settle in on a generation of pine needles, a soft sweet bed of decay. Fear has surrendered to response.

At nine, I'm drunk on the smell of wet piney soil, the taste of the night sky, and the wandering dance of the moon, barely glimpsed through the pine boughs.

I'm spinning. I'm flat on my back, fingers clutching the soil. But I'm spinning. Starlight, moonlight, my light. Spinning. Threads of light spin together. I see the weaving in and out of the light, creating light, creating form.

I hear the big red cur dog bark again. Three times, he barks. Then the shuffle of shod hooves on a straw-lined stable floor.

When I open my eyes (when did I close them?), I see that owl again. This time she settles on a branch far above me, with something in her beak. I'm home again, and now face the long dark walk back to my bed.

I suppose they're still asleep, Mom and Dad.

FLIGHT OF THE CRONE

SMOKY TRUDEAU

Face to the sun, arms outstretched
crone takes to the skies, free.
She soars over prairie, the
raven and hawk her companions.
They race. Crone wins.
Rooted in the earth, big bluestem, compass plant
reach for the sky, longing to join her.

REFLECTED FEAR

MILENA GOMEZ

The reflection in the mirror
looked back at me
in fear.
Within my own skin
I was shaking,
dejected.

Once, I was standing still,
yielding to my failures,
my regrets.
Afraid the world
would see me,
rejected.

In abandon, my eyes
moved past the mirror.
Life's stage was waiting,
in motion.

My insecurities
were stripped away.

The reflection in the mirror
did not survive.
Courage replaced it.
Within my own skin
I was overcome
by praises.

Now, I no longer
stand still.
The reflected fear
is shaken.
I am the mirror
where fear is reflected,
dejected,
rejected.

WIDE OPEN

L. E. HARVEY

Anne was a bright, energetic young woman. At only 5 feet tall, she was a little stick of dynamite. She would dance around the house like it was the stage of the New York City Ballet. She openly claimed the "Oscar Meyer Weiner" song as her own personal theme song. She had the ability to take anyone's name and use it in place of "Lola" in Barry Manilow's "Copa Cabanna." With Anne's Broadway style singing, the people around her enjoyed these humorous songs with even greater appreciation. Like most people in their mid-twenties, she desired to enjoy every moment of life. The people in her life, however, made sure to quell that energy and box her in.

Anne came from a strict Catholic family. Her parents were knighted in the Catholic Church. They had more religious connections than the Pope himself. Anne was currently seeing a young man named Michael, who came from a strict Baptist family. Their religious zeal was more than overwhelming at times for Anne. The blatant differences between the 2 families simply added confusion and stress for Anne. No matter which family she visited, no matter whom she spoke to, she always had to watch what she said, how she acted, who she was. There was judgment and prejudice in both families due to their religious affiliations. Anne stood out like a sore thumb in both families.

Anne was a heavily tattooed and pierced biker. Her naturally raven-colored hair made her appear almost gothic. She was openly bi-sexual. She could make a sailor blush with her language. Anne followed a belief system called Wicca. It was an uncommon "religion." It followed many of the ancient civilizations' beliefs, but was very respectful and accepting of any and all beliefs systems. Despite her unique beliefs and lifestyle, Anne was always sure to remain "closeted" when discussing religion or politics with either family. Anne was unique and loud, but still very respectful to all the people in her life. That was a trait that Michael greatly appreciated in his girlfriend.

Anne and Michael had long been friends, and knew much of each other, and the other's family. Like Anne, although Michael came from a strict family, he, and his beliefs were independent. He accepted her for who she was; he respected her beliefs and her lifestyle. Their relationship was strong, and was based on mutual respect.

Both families accepted Anne, and their relationship, simply out of obligation. Her parents had to: she was their daughter. Michael's family had to, there was already talk of marriage. Neither family had any issue, though, expressing their disappointment in her, or passing judgment on someone who they considered to be anything but a good Christian. Anne took it in stride, feeling that she was "too much" for anyone to fully understand.

One cold, frozen, January day, Anne's life shattered like a fallen icicle. Michael drastically changed. He suddenly had a rage-full side to him that she had never seen before. She didn't know if she had said the wrong thing, looked at him the wrong way, or what the cause might have been. Regardless, she was no longer a person, she was a punching bag. Now, not only did Anne need to hide her tattoos around the families, she needed to hide the bruises as well.

Convicted by her love and devotion for Michael, and well as her strong Catholic-rooted beliefs in the finality of marriage, she and Michael sought counsel from his family's pastor. For months, they met as a couple, and individually with the pastor. They read books, they talked. Like any abusive relationship, though, there were phenomenal times, and phenomenally horrific times. The counseling helped on occasion, but the beatings never truly stopped.

If you looked at Anne, you'd never suspect that she would allow herself to be beaten. Anne could walk down the street and mothers would clutch their children tightly in fear of her presence. Anne was an expert at hiding her reality.

Finally, she had taken the last hit, literally. Anne called the local police while hiding in the closet in the spare bedroom. Fearful for her life, she didn't know where else to turn. While still on the phone with dispatch, there was a loud pounding on the door. The police had finally arrived.

Two very large and intimidating officers entered the house. Anne's tough exterior was long gone. For the first time, Anne saw that even Michael was intimidated by these other men. One cop ushered Michael upstairs to speak to him privately, the other remained downstairs to speak with Anne. She told him the stories of the abuse, the counseling, all of it. The police officer gave her information for women's shelters, domestic violence hotlines, and more. Anne backed away a bit to better read the papers from the officer. When she looked up, she saw Michael being escorted out the door with both large police officers. The door shut behind them. It was the loudest, harshest door slam Anne had ever heard.

Within days, Anne had a new place. Knowing that Michael would soon be returning, since Anne had only filed a police report and didn't press charges, she had no choice but to move quickly. She grabbed all of her belongings and moved it all in just one night. After it was over, she exhaustedly looked around the new apartment with boxes strewn all over, and she took in a deep breath of freedom.

By the time her first month in the new apartment had come to an end, there was a gay pride sticker on her car. Her house was decorated to her taste, not in some way to please someone else. Anne began to dance around the house again. She gladly belted out show tunes in the shower. Anne had been released from her captive box.

Several months after leaving Michael, Anne decided to branch out and meet new people. Anne felt the time had come to bring new people, and new joy, into her life. Co-workers, new friends with similar interests, and neighbors had begun to add real color to the tapestry of Anne's life. She eventually met someone, a girl named Shannon. They met through mutual friends and instantly connected. Shannon was cute and flirtatious; it was hard for Anne to resist. Anne wanted to take things with Shannon slowly, though. Shannon fully understood and respected Anne's history, and allowed her new girlfriend to set the pace for their budding relationship. Big changes were taking place in Anne's life.

One small, yet very ironic element remained, though. Anne continued to read the Bible on her own. She knew that the 2 extremes from which she had just come needed to meet somewhere in the middle.

After much reading and deep reflection, Anne knew that God loved her just as she was: tattoos, piercings, sexuality, "Oscar Meyer Weiner" song, and all. She was who she was supposed to be. She could finally revel in her own identity and know that the higher power accepted her as such. She understood that in true Christianity (in any religion, really), God loved Anne for who and what she was. The higher power would never try to quell such a bright, energetic spirit. Anne had begun to embrace herself, and her life with arms wide open.

THE TIES THAT UNBIND

VICTORIA HOWARD

Emma pulled the crumpled letter from her pocket and checked the address on Primrose Drive. After hours of walking through the tree-lined streets, she'd finally found the right one. Her steps slowed as she checked the house numbers, looking for eighty-six.

Built to accommodate factory workers during the Industrial Revolution, the newly-renovated row of red-bricked Victorian terraced cottages, in the fashionable Cotswold town, looked sleek and smart in the autumn sunshine. Old fashioned wooden doors and windows had been replaced, for the most part, by modern double-glazing. The front gardens were carefully landscaped and full of shrubs and flowers.

Emma's hand tightened on the strap of her bag. After all these years of waiting, she suddenly felt nervous. Her hand trembled as she opened the gate, and walked down the block-paved path towards the oak-panelled door. She straightened her suit jacket, ran a hand through her hair, then lifted the brass door knocker.

A dog barked. Taking a deep, unsteady breath, Emma stepped back. She hated dogs no matter what their breed or size. Through the door she heard a high-pitched female voice yell at the dog, then the unmistakable sound of a bolt being drawn.

The door opened a couple of inches.

A small, gray-haired woman peered through the narrow gap. "If you're selling something you can walk away now, because whatever it is, we don't want it."

"Wait!" Emma called. "Please don't close the door. I'm looking for Margaret Royal. She used to live at number thirteen Bank Street, in Liverpool."

The woman's eyes narrowed as she looked Emma up and down. "Why? And how do you know my name?"

Emma swallowed nervously. "The Adoption Society gave it to me. I'm her...I'm your daughter. I'm Emma."

From somewhere within the house a male voice called. "Who is it Margaret?"

The woman turned her head and shouted over her shoulder. "It's just someone selling double glazing." To Emma she said, "You've got the wrong Mrs Royal. I've never lived in Liverpool, and I don't have a daughter."

Emma stared at the woman. She knew she was lying. Even she could see the similarities—the intense blue eyes, the nose that titled up at the end, and the high cheek bones.

"I'm your daughter and I can prove it. I don't want anything, just ten minutes of your time. I just...I just want to ask you to some questions, that's all. May I come in?"

"I've told you, you've got the wrong woman. Now, go away before I call the police."

"Look, I understand it must be difficult with me turning up out of the blue. It's probably not something you wish to discuss on the doorstep. I'm staying at the Dog and Fox in Market Square until Thursday. Ask for Emma Rothchild."

The woman said nothing, merely closed the door.

Emma turned and re-traced her steps. She needed time to think. She walked back through the narrow streets to her hotel, impervious to the rain soaking through the thin fabric of her jacket, and the stares of the passersby.

No matter how cold hearted Margaret Royal was, she was till her mother, and she couldn't go home without trying to talk to her one more time.

It had taken her ten long years of searching to finally track down her mother. Margaret Royal and her husband never stayed in one place for very long. Five times Emma had located her, only to find that Margaret Royal had either moved without a forwarding address, or had seemingly disappeared without trace. It was only through painstaking searches of the electoral roll, marriage, and divorce records, that she'd finally been able to track her down.

The fact that her mother changed names almost as often as Emma had changed jobs hadn't helped her search. In the last five years alone, Margaret had changed her name from Collins, to Evans, and finally to Royal, making Emma speculate just what her mother was trying to hide.

Back in her hotel room, Emma showered and changed, then ordered room service. While she waited for the pot of coffee and sandwich to arrive, she lifted her briefcase onto the bed, and pulled out a manila folder. She opened it and took out a faded photograph, its surface cracked and torn from years of handling. A petite girl in a yellow dress, her blonde hair tied back in pigtails, sat next to a young woman on a picnic rug, and smiled for the camera. She clearly remembered the day it was taken.

Emma and her mother, had joined her best friend Jane, for the annual Sunday school outing. They'd sat in the back of the coach and had laughed and sung "Knick, knack, paddywhack," all the way from Liverpool to North Wales. Around lunchtime, the coach had stopped on the moors above Llanberis, and they'd eaten their picnic lunch of ham sandwiches and sausage rolls. That was when Jane had taken the photo.

It had been the happiest day of Emma's young life.

Two days later, the day before her seventh birthday, she'd come home from school to find the house empty and her mother gone.

At first she thought her mother had nipped to the shops and forgotten to leave a note, but when she didn't come home that night and the one after that, Emma realised her mother was never coming back.

She'd gone to bed frightened and confused.

The next morning she'd dressed and gone to school as usual. By the end of the week she'd eaten what little food there was in the fridge and had resorted to stealing. It was only when Mr Jones, their next door neighbour, caught Emma taking the milk and eggs off his doorstep, did anyone realise that she was on her own.

After that her memories were vague. There was the woman from Social Services, then the nightmare of the children's home, of being stripped and made to wear a uniform, the dreadful food, the constant crying, and the endless bullying and abuse by the older children.

The smiling seven-year old in the photograph had vanished to be replaced by a quiet, withdrawn child. Even now, twenty-five years later, she could recall every one of the foster homes she been placed in. The promise that her 'new parents' would love and treat as their own child had never been fulfilled. Nor had she forgotten the overwhelming sense of relief she'd felt on her eighteenth birthday, when she'd finally been able to leave their care and make her own way in the world.

Emma carefully replaced the photograph in the folder alongside a tattered piece of cotton that had once been a handkerchief, and snapped it shut. A hot tear ran down her cheek. Years of therapy had done little to wipe out the memories of abandonment and desolation she'd felt as a child, just as nothing could stop her despising the woman who'd given birth to her thirty-two years previously.

She crossed the room to the window and rested her face against the cold, rain-washed glass. Trapped by the memory of her emotions, she struggled to understand why a mother would abandon her child.

"Why? Why did you leave me alone?" she whispered.

She'd gone to the house today in the hope of hearing the answer to that question and to find peace of mind. She wasn't interested in knowing if her mother had won the lottery or married a millionaire.

The telephone on the bedside table rang, making her jump.

"Hello?"

"There's a Mrs Royal in reception, asking for you."

"Thank you. Ask her to wait in the lounge. I'll be there in a moment."

Emma checked her appearance in the mirror, then snatched the folder and her room key off the table, and went downstairs.

Her mother sat in a corner, her hands neatly folded in her lap. She appeared small and frail, and Emma wondered why she hadn't noticed that earlier.

"Thank you for coming," she said, sitting down in the chair next to her. "Would you like some tea or a drink perhaps?"

"No, thanks. I haven't got long. John, my husband, thinks I've gone to Church to help with the flower arrangements. Let me get straight to the point. I'm not saying I've a daughter, mind you, but if I did, what makes you so certain you're her?"

Emma opened the folder. "This," she said holding up the photograph. "It is you, isn't it?"

Margaret Royal stared at the photograph and was silent for a long moment. Her face, albeit much younger, smiled back at her. She closed her eyes, the sadness clearly visible on her face. "Who gave you this?"

"My best friend, Jane. She'd borrowed her brother's camera. Don't you remember? I fell over just after it was taken and you cleaned my knee with your handkerchief." She held out the square of cotton. "Why did you abandon me?"

Margaret took it, and pressed it to her cheek. "You were too young to understand. Your father..." she looked away. "Your father left me the moment he found out I was pregnant—said you weren't his. I'd never been with another man. I had no choice but to try and bring you up myself. It was a struggle, but I worked for as long as I could. The day after you were born your father came to see me. He gave me some money, enough take out a lease on a small terraced house, and to put some aside for emergencies. As soon as I could I sent you to nursery, and went back to work."

"What about my grandparents? Couldn't they have helped?"

"They were ashamed of me and didn't want anything to do with me. At first I managed, but you grew so quick, always needing new clothes, new shoes. Eventually all the money had gone, and I struggled to pay the rent. The landlord threatened to evict us, and there was nowhere else we could go. I thought..." Margaret lowered her gaze. "I thought that if I left you, Social Services would take you into care and find a nice foster family for you, someone who could love you and give you all the things I couldn't. I couldn't cope with a young child anymore."

Emma signalled a waiter for some tea.

"Have you any idea what it was like coming home and finding you gone? Can you imagine how scared I was? How alone I felt? I thought I'd done something terribly wrong and you were punishing me for being naughty. And as for me being placed in a nice foster family, nothing could be further than the truth. I had nine sets of foster parents. Nine! Each time I moved to another house, another family, I thought this will be great; they'll love me and care for me. But they didn't. I became an inconvenience, a way for them to earn extra money. After a while, they'd get fed up of having me around, and I'd be moved to another home. And another. Until I reached my eighteenth birthday and was free to look after myself."

Margaret set her chin in a stubborn line. "I knew you wouldn't understand. That's why I never tried to make contact. I knew that once you came of age you had the right to try and find me. But I hoped—no prayed—that you wouldn't."

Emma felt her temper rise. She took a deep breath to steady herself. "That's rather selfish of you. Where did you go after you left?"

"Birmingham, at first. I got a job working in a factory. As soon as I'd saved enough money I went to London. But I didn't like it there, so I moved back to Liverpool. After a while, I met someone. He was a nice chap. A sailor. We were together for a few years, until he was killed in a road accident. There were a couple of other men, but none of them stayed around for long. I met my current husband two years ago."

"It's taken me a long time to find you."

"Then you should have spent your time more wisely. I haven't got any money, if that's what you're after."

"I don't want your money. But I can't just walk away without trying to get to know you. Aren't you just a little bit curious to know what sort of woman I've grown into? Whether I'm happy and have a good job."

"You're part of my life I want to forget."

Emma waited until the waiter left the tea tray on the table before replying. "You'd wouldn't be here, if that were true. So, why have you come?"

"To tell you to stay away. John, well, John has a bit of a temper. He hates children. I've never told him much about my past, so I don't want you interfering in my life."

"I have no intention of interfering, as you put it. But I am curious to know what sort of mother turns her back on her child."

"It wasn't easy, but it was for the best."

"For you maybe, but certainly not for me. Did you ever stop to think how your actions might affect me psychologically? Do you know how hard it was growing up knowing your mother didn't love you; that your parents weren't really your parents, at all?"

"You were six, for God's sake. I thought you'd forget about me."

"I was nearly seven. And not a day goes by without me thinking about you. Can you imagine how difficult it's been for me to learn to love, to trust, to believe in someone?"

"Lots of children are abandoned. You weren't the first, and you certainly won't be the last. They manage to get on with their lives. So stop trying to make me feel guilty."

"I'm sorry, I didn't come here to make you feel guilty. I came because I wanted to get to know you."

"That's not going to happen, so you may as well pack your bag and go back to wherever you came from."

"But don't you want to know if I'm married, whether I have children—whether you have grandchildren?"

"Grandchildren! They're the last thing I want to be saddled with. John and I travel a great deal. We don't want grandchildren mucking up our lives. Now, if you don't mind, I've wasted enough time talking to you. I'd better be going."

Emma watched dumbfounded as her mother stood. "I'm sorry you won't give us the chance to get to know each other. If you should change your mind at any time, this where you can contact me." Emma held out her business card.

Margaret Royal ignored the card. "Please, forget about me. Be happy, and get on with your life. And whatever you do, don't try to contact me again."

Emma hand rested gently on her stomach as watched her mother walk away, determined that her child would have all the love she could give it.

SEASON FOR LOVE

JACQUELINE SEEWALD

London, England, 1809

"The Season is very much like the war being waged against Bonaparte," Lady Deidre Audley explained to Drucilla, taking a moment to select a sugar plum and pop it into her mouth with her plump fingers. "There are numerous battles that need to be fought strategically, but one will not win them unless attention is paid to the veriest detail in each skirmish."

Drucilla gave her mama an apathetic sigh. "I am beautiful. Everyone says so. Do they not?" She looked to Caroline for affirmation. "Therefore, it does not signify that I must plot like some inferior creature. It is quite beneath me. I shall be accounted a great success regardless."

"I have nursed the ground for you, and your wardrobe is in the first stare of fashion. However, London is not the country, my girl. You will not be considered a diamond of the first water immediately. I learned that many years ago when I had my first season. There will be many beauties of noble family, high birth and heritage as well as great wealth. You may be sought after, my dear, but we are looking for someone with deep pockets. There is always competition in that regard. You have much to learn about the marriage mart."

"Yes, Mama." Drucilla rolled her lovely eyes.

Caroline continued working on her composition at the pianoforte. This discussion was of little consequence to her. Of course, she would have liked to be part of it, but that did not signify. As Mama had explained, all efforts must be concentrated on providing Drucilla with the best opportunity to make an unobjectionable match. Caroline would remain in the background--nor was a fashionable wardrobe possible for her since all resources were to be centered on Drucilla.

Papa had died before Drucilla could have her come-out. Now that the year of mourning had passed, Drucilla would finally be shown to advantage. Mama was especially concerned, because Drucilla was soon to turn nineteen, and most of the girls being introduced into society would be seventeen. Caroline was herself eighteen, but it was unlikely that she would have a Season of her own.

Stevens, the long-nosed butler, entered the drawing room. Like the rest of the servants, except for Mama and Drucilla's personal maids, he had been rented for the Season along with the house itself. Stevens extended a silver tray that held calling cards.

"You have visitors, Madam."

Mama smiled, her pleasure evident. "Please show them in. We are receiving this afternoon. Have Cook prepare high tea."

Caroline knew very well there would not have been tea otherwise. Mama was quite frugal. Many things were just for appearances. Papa's estate had been entailed and passed to a distant cousin. Mama was no longer the wife of a baronet. Papa's personal wealth had been considerably diminished by poor investments and gaming. But Mama explained that it was important that no one else knew of their difficult financial circumstances. She had no intention of fading into shabby gentility.

Mama needed little excuse to ignore Caroline. Mama had little regard for her partly because she had been born female. Both her parents were bitterly disappointed that there was no heir. Caroline had once been present when Mama told her friend, Lady Judith, how the doctor explained all was not well after Caroline's birth. There would be no more children. Caroline was aware that Mama blamed her for this major disappointment. Papa's attitude had been similar. As Mama had bitterly pointed out, unlike Drucilla, Caroline was not even beautiful. Her appearance was plain. Lady Judith was all that was sympathetic.

It seemed that Lady Judith was visiting today. The old friends, who had not been in touch for some time, regarded each other fondly. But they had something in common that drew them closer together: each lady was a widow.

"Dear Judith," Mama said warmly as her friend entered the elegantly appointed room, "so good of you to come. And who have you brought with you?"

"My two nephews," Lady Judith said. "This is Lord William Stafford, the Earl of Renwood, and Lord Gregory Stafford, his brother."

The Earl was a beefy man with a ruddy complexion and butter-colored hair. He had small, dull eyes; Caroline did not find him at all interesting. But his brother, Lord Gregory, that was a different matter entirely. The younger man was a soldier, a military officer who looked splendid in his scarlet uniform. He had broad shoulders and lean hips. His facial expression was animated, eyes sky blue with a twinkle. She vowed she'd never seen anyone so handsome! But it was more than looks. There was an energy, a vitality humming about him.

Both gentlemen were introduced to Drucilla whose interest was immediately drawn to the Earl. Caroline observed and listened intently. It was clear to her that Lady Judith had conspired with Mama to introduce Drucilla to an eligible *parti*.

"Do you like hunting?" The earl asked Drucilla.

"I am not accustomed to the outdoors. It is bad for the complexion," Drucilla responded with an air of superior knowledge.

"Pity," the earl mumbled. "Don't suppose you fish either?"

"Catch those slimy, smelly things? Decidedly not."

"Perhaps you might take Drucilla for a ride in your carriage tomorrow. Renwood has a splendid conveyance," Lady Judith observed.

"Through the park in the afternoon?" Drucilla brightened.

"As you wish," the Earl agreed.

After that, the conversation came more easily. Lord Gregory turned from Drucilla and looked in Caroline's direction. One golden brow rose quizzically. He joined her at the piano bench.

"And who might you be? Not a maid obviously. Are you a relation?"

She colored, knowing what he must be thinking. How poorly turned out she was in her drab, gray wool dress! She was ashamed of her shabby appearance. Her hair was unfashionably long and worn down at Mama's insistence, to make it look as if she were still a schoolgirl.

"I am Drucilla's sister, Caroline."

He looked surprised. "You are not yet out I take it."

Nor was it likely she would ever be.

"Still in school?"

"I was, but my teachers felt I had learned all they had to offer." In fact, she'd been teaching the younger girls at the seminary until Mama pulled her out. The Misses Bowens who ran the school would have been delighted to employ her to teacher art and music to the lower levels, but Mama was incensed when the offer of employment arose. Mama explained that women of a certain class did not under any circumstances take menial positions. Caroline had loved working with the girls. She let out a deep sigh of regret now as she recalled it.

"Play for me?" Lord Gregory asked.

Caroline obliged him with a country air. When he began to sing in a deep baritone voice, she could not resist joining in. Everyone stopped talking to listen. The Earl begged them to continue performing, which they did for another half hour.

Everyone was pleased but Mama. Caroline saw her mother glower at her and quickly stopped.

When it was time to leave, Lord Gregory turned to his brother. "William, I believe we must invite Lady Caroline to join us in our outing tomorrow."

"That would not be proper," Mama quickly said. "My younger daughter is not yet out."

"I have no proper clothes to wear," Caroline admitted.

"Aunt, isn't Matilda just about the same size as Miss Audley?" Lord Gregory inquired.

"Yes, I shall have some appropriate things sent over," Lady Judith agreed. Matilda was only sixteen, but Caroline was actually smaller in size.

Caroline was embarrassed and certain Mama was fuming. But she found it impossible to refuse. Lord Gregory was simply too dynamic and vital.

The following day, Caroline found herself being driven along Rotten Row in an open carriage sitting in back with Lord Gregory. Drucilla sat decorously beside the Earl who held the reins.

"I say, you clean up rather well," Renwood observed as he turned to study Caroline.

She felt herself color from her hairline to her neck.

"What William means is that we are honored by the company of two such lovely young ladies," Lord Gregory said with more tact. "We must thank Aunt Judith for the introduction."

"Quite so," the Earl agreed. He took off at a fast pace, unsuited to the sedate riding of those who came to the park to see and be seen.

"Do slow down!" Drucilla said crossly.

"Forgot myself," Renwood said. "I'm a bit of a dab with the ribbons."

"William is accustomed to racing his curricle," Lord Gregory explained.

Drucilla straightened her bonnet huffily.

"Perhaps we might walk for a bit," Caroline suggested. "The park is so lovely today."

And so the two couples walked and chatted somewhat separately, and Caroline forgot that there was anyone else in the world except the handsome young officer. It seemed they never ran out of things to talk about. She thought Lord Gregory possessed of a clever wit. They laughed together, and Caroline found herself sparkling for the first time in her life.

"You are quite extraordinary," Lord Gregory said, staring into her eyes, "so unspoiled, a beautiful girl, inside and out."

"I assure you, I am quite ordinary. But your manner is so amiable, you would bring out the best in anybody."

For just a moment, they were separated from public view, hidden from curious eyes by a large piece of shrubbery. Lord Gregory pulled Caroline into his arms, an intense expression on his face. All words stopped. Language seemed inadequate. Lord Gregory brushed her lips with his own. His lips were cool and gentle, but then the kiss became more demanding.

Caroline knew in her mind that she should not respond with anything resembling a welcome. Any encouragement of such behavior was totally inappropriate. That had been drilled into her. One must exercise decorum, always do what was proper. And yet she found herself responding to him with such deep passionate feeling, wanting more of

Gregory. Her pulse raced and she could scarcely breathe. She had never been so overwhelmed by emotion. Surely, there was no more wonderful, exciting man in the entire world! She kissed him back with arms wide open. She gave of herself, holding nothing back.

"Caroline, Lord Gregory! Where are you?"

Drucilla was almost upon them. They pulled apart guiltily. Before they returned to the carriage, Gregory spoke to her in a soft urgent voice meant for her ears alone.

"Lady Caroline, I most humbly apologize for acting less than a gentleman. I generally show courtesy toward a lady. But I was overcome by the most powerful longing. You must think me a wretched cad."

She shook her head, not trusting herself to speak. Finally, words came haltingly.

"I felt exactly the same way. I will not deny my true feelings."

He squeezed her hand. "I would like to know you better. However, tomorrow I leave for Portugal. I join my regiment to fight there. Hopefully, we will trounce Boney once and for all."

"Tomorrow? So soon?" She felt an actual pain in the vicinity of her heart.

He nodded sadly. "Afraid so."

"I hope this will not sound too forward, but may I write to you?"

"Of course, and I will write when I can as well."

"I will always remember you," she said. She felt the tears well up in her eyes and blinked them back.

Lord Gregory continued to hold her hand, clasping it tightly. "Dear girl, you will have your own Season soon enough and forget all about me."

Caroline simply smiled and shook her head emphatically. "I will never forget you."

ঽঽঽ

Yorkshire, England, 1811

Lady Judith dropped her embroidery, her face lighting up with pleasure, as her nephew was announced. "Gregory, you are home!"

Caroline watched him limp into the room, resting heavily on a walking stick for support. His eyes met hers directly. He looked pale and gaunt, a ghost of the vital young man she remembered.

"Gregory, you did not let us know that you were wounded." Lady Judith took her arm.

He shrugged. "I thought it best not to do so. You could do nothing about it and the knowledge would only upset you."

"My nerves do not overset easily," Lady Judith scolded. "You stopped writing, you bad boy."

"I had little worth saying." His expression was grim.

"We should have liked knowing about what was happening in the Peninsular War."

"Wellington is making progress. Hopefully we'll soon be on to Spain." He turned to Caroline. "Are you visiting?"

Caroline shook her head, unable to speak.

"Caroline has come to live with me at Fairhaven. I have been lonely since Matilda married."

"What about Lady Audley? Does she not object to you taking over her daughter?"

Caroline trained her eyes on the Aubusson carpet. "Mama lives with Drucilla and her husband. They are soon to be blessed by a child."

"A shame Drucilla and William did not take," Lady Judith said with a deep sigh. She turned back to Gregory. "Drucilla married Lord Severn. He was a widower with two children. He was so delighted to have a young, beautiful wife that he spoils Drucilla shamelessly. He positively dotes on her, constantly presenting her with outrageously expensive gifts. My dear friend cannot say enough in praise of the generosity of her son-in-law. She adores him."

"I am glad for them," Lord Gregory said politely.

"Indeed, it is just as well that Drucilla did not take with your brother, what with his untimely passing."

"What exactly happened? The letter sent by the solicitor merely informed me that there was an accident."

"Indeed, he was racing madly when the curricle went over a cliff. His friends claimed he'd been drinking and his judgment was impaired."

"May I express my condolences," Caroline said in a quiet, subdued voice.

Lady Judith saw the look that passed between Caroline and Gregory. "Well, I must be off to talk with Cook about our dinner menu. You, of course, will stay with us before you take up your new duties."

They hardly noticed when Lady Judith left the room.

"Does your injury hurt very much?" Caroline asked. He was still very handsome, but there were lines etched into his face.

"One gets used to it," he said with stoicism.

"Why did you not write?" She kept her voice cool.

"I did intend to do so at first, but then I lost the words. I would have said unpleasant things, written only about the war."

"I thought my letters were not reaching you, or worse still, that you wanted nothing more to do with me. Perhaps I presumed too much."

He looked up, his blue eyes meeting her own dark ones. "That was never the case. In fact, you were rarely out of my thoughts."

"But I did not know that," she said quietly.

"What of your Season? Did you have it?"

She shook her head.

Gregory rose angrily to his feet. "How cruel to deny you that! I shall talk to my aunt about the matter, rest assured!"

Caroline put her hand on his sleeve. "No, you do not understand. I did not wish it."

He stared at her in surprise. "Why not?"

She bit her lower lip. This was not going to be easy. "The fact is, my heart was taken."

He turned her to face him. "By whom?"

"A British officer who I hoped would return my affections. In any case, I could love no other."

"Oh, Caroline, I do not deserve such devotion!"

Her throat was too choked with emotion to allow her to speak. With the utmost embarrassment, she burst into tears. Gregory took her into his arms and rubbed her back soothingly.

"My dear, sweet girl, I've brought you so much unhappiness. I truly regret that. You must forget me now. My aunt will see that you make a good match."

"You do not want me? I was afraid it was so."

He held her tightly. "Not so. But I am lame, a cripple. There was a time when I thought I would lose my leg entirely. I told the surgeon I would prefer to die, and so I hovered between life and death for quite a while, out of my mind from fever and infection. I would never ask you to spend your life burdened with an invalid like myself."

"I will have no other man," she said firmly. "But it does not signify because I am not good enough for you. I have no dowry to offer. An earl can look much higher. Your aunt has been kind enough to welcome me into her household as an unofficial companion. I am content. She has treated me better than my own family ever did."

"Oh, Caroline, I do not want any other woman. I have loved you from the moment we met."

This time the kiss that passed between them ignited with overwhelming passion. To touch this man again, to feel his lips touch hers, was too much. Fire burned through her blood. She trembled with want and need for him.

When at last they caught their breath, Gregory caressed her cheek. "I shall apply for a special license immediately, darling. We have wasted enough time. We will not be apart again."

Caroline felt an overwhelming joy. She had risked everything for love and had no regrets.

The Cafeteria

Sarah Natalia Lee

"I don't know why Mr. Jameson is such a freak. I mean, really. Giving an exam like that right after *spring break*. What did he expect us to do, conjugate *sum* and all its crazy friends every night? *Possum, absum,* and what was that other one that sounds like *absum*?"

Anna never shuts up about how much she hates Latin. Criticizing the language that is responsible for nearly every language spoken in Europe is like her only hobby. No, not just hobby, *obsession.*

"How am *I* supposed to know?" Meghan says.

"*Adsum?*" I throw out.

"Yeah, that one. God, I hate that class so much."

"Well at least you're not taking Greek, like my *boyfriend,*" Miss Melodie I-Have-A-Boyfriend-Aren't-I-Hot says. "He says it's the hardest class in the *world.*"

"So what'd everyone do this weekend?" Rapid change of subject is a natural dynamic of high school conversation. Actually, it's more like a law of physics. Newton's fourth law. An object maintains its velocity unless acted on by an unbalanced outside force, net force equals mass times acceleration, every action has an equal and opposite reaction, and high schoolers' conversations are as unpredictable as the school lunch menu.

"My stupid mother forced me to see this dumb movie because my brother wanted to go. God, it was so *lame*." Shawna leans back in her chair and twists and untwists the cap on her bottle of water.

"Really? I hung out with Jenni at the mall." Anna's off the Latin-bashing, at least for the current five seconds.

"I spent it at my boyfriend's." Melodie again.

This is the moment I decide to let my mind wander. My eyes stray across the crowded cafeteria...and come to rest on the abandoned form of the school pariah.

Eleanor McCormick. Sitting alone at a table in the corner, waiting for the lunch lines to die down. Not a soul beside her. Not a pair of eyes on her.

Eleanor isn't ugly. She isn't geeky or cursed with acne. Her hair is a mass of long, cascading red curls, and her outfits are always very colorful and coordinated. She kind of looks like an Irish princess, really. And she's quiet, not the sort of annoying loudmouth who automatically makes everyone hate her, like I tend to be. I've only spoken to her once; I was standing beside the glass doors to the art wing when she came up. She smiled at me; I nodded in response. Then she reached for the door and flung it open, a bit too hard, I might add, because it slammed me straight in the nose. "Yeep!"

And Eleanor, in her eternal concern for the well-being of anyone but herself, flew right back through the door and was on top of me before I even had a chance to open my eyes.

"Omigawd! Are you okay? I'm so sorry!"

I nodded again, massaging my pulsing nose. She cocked her head and furrowed her brow. "Are you sure?"

"Yeah, honey, I'm fine. Don't worry about it."

"Okay." She hesitantly turned and walked back through the door. We never spoke again, but each time I passed her in the halls I allowed myself that tiny smile.

No, Eleanor's the sort of girl who could be very popular if it weren't for the one thing that's holding her back in this conservative, small-town rural school.

She's the only lesbian here. I mean, I'm sure there are others, but she's the only one who was unfortunate enough to be caught kissing Yvonne Packard in the girls' restroom during lunch right before Christmas break. By the giggliest, most gossipy girl in school, no less. Having already gotten all of her credits, Yvonne graduated ten days later, so she was kinda off scot-free. But it's another story for poor Eleanor McCormick, who lost all her friends and still has three painful semesters to kill off before she can fly away.

And so she's the scapegoat for every geek, heathen, and misfit here. You could walk in wearing headgear, a mullet, and taped-up 1950's glasses and attract less criticism than Eleanor. At least you don't sleep with the *same sex*.

"Why are you staring at Lezzie Leslie?"

I turn back. Meghan's inquiring eyes are burning a hole through me.

"Her name's Eleanor, Meghan."

"Oh, well, *you* would know."

"That's not funny, Meghan."

"Yeah it is!" This from Mitchell, my ex.

"My boyfriend would think it's hilarious."

Oh, just shut up about your boyfriend already! The only reason I even sit with these people is because my best friends, Trisha and Sean, do. And sometimes I wonder if the only reason they do is because they have nowhere else to eat. Well, there's plenty of room at Eleanor's table. But who wants all that bad publicity?

I glance back to Eleanor. She's leaving, headed for the now empty lunch line. My eyes follow her up to the bar, past the huge beverage machine, and through the cashier. Her flimsy little Styrofoam tray (note to self: write to principal about the environmental consequences of going through over 1700 Styrofoam trays a week) is laden now with spaghetti and mixed veggies. She starts back to her table, working hard not to drop anything from her overflowing tray. As she passes my table, Rob Daniels, who is sitting at the next table over, reaches his foot and trips her. With a little shriek, she falls, her food flying like a dog shaking off water.

The cafeteria erupts in cacophonous laughter. Everyone around me is hysterical; even Trisha and Sean are laughing. Pain shoots through my heart as I watch poor Eleanor kneel there, not even bothering to gather her pre-packaged items. I should help her.

With a third of the school watching? Then *I* would be a pariah. Everyone would ostracize me, too, and they'd think I was her girlfriend or something. Even Sean and Trisha might refuse to speak to me. My mom once said, "A friend who leaves you for doing the right thing is of no more worth than a childhood toy." Maybe so, but Sean and Trisha are kind of like my lifelines at this school. Is it worth all that pain to make one person feel better?

Eleanor finally moves, slowly reaching for her Powerade bottle. I hear some gay slurs blast around me. One person. One innocent, lonely person, who probably cries herself to sleep every night, praying for just one friend, one ally in the place that used to be her home. I remember a line from the fifth Harry Potter movie, which I saw last summer. *The time has come to choose between what is right and what is easy.*

I must decide what to do. Now. It's incredible how much of your life can hang on a moment, isn't it? But as Eleanor looks up, at all the cruelty, at all the laughing faces, the faces of my supposed friends, I see a single tear trickle over her freckled cheek. And my mind is made up.

I step forward and bend down.

"Hey. Let me help you with that."

THE COLOR OF CHANGE

KATE EVANS

The first time I woke up next to a woman was in a hotel bed. It was dawn, faint light eking in along the edges of the thick hotel curtains.

She was asleep, her body on the edge of illumination. The previous morning, like all the times in my life I had slept with a lover, dawn revealed a man next to me. Now here lay a woman, fleshy arm, shadowy dimples on her thigh, press of breast against the pillow. This womanly contrast was made stronger by the memory, the visceral echo, of my boyfriend's bony angularity.

My boyfriend, a scientist who worked late into the night in his lab, didn't want me to make noise in the apartment until noon. I blow-dried my hair in the kitchen, brushed my teeth over last night's dinner dishes in the aluminum sink, and pulled the living-room curtains slowly across the rod.

I watched the sun rise, glowing orange into the blue swimming pool. If he woke up before noon, I wasn't to say "good morning" because he'd feel obligated to reply. He didn't want to speak until he was ready. As he put it, it took him time to unthaw.

It wasn't only mornings that he didn't want to talk, though. Sometimes when he fell into his self-described "black moods," he'd turn on the TV, don headphones blasting Led Zepplin, and sit on the couch, slowly turning the pages of a book on Leonardo da Vinci.

A Leonardo scholar, he not only collected books about Leonardo, he also collected incunabula—books published before 1500. His goal was to own a copy of every book Leonardo was believed to have read. This was his hobby, when he wasn't doing whatever it was he did with proteins in the lab. ("Your boyfriend's going to win the Nobel Prize one day," one of his lab buddies once said.)

Dawn with David shed light on my aloneness. When I woke not to his face but to a pillow over his head, when I climbed gingerly out of bed so as to not touch him or make a sound, I knew that more than a pillow separated us.

He was an East Coast intellectual who couldn't wait to get out of California, once his post-doc was finished; I was a California native who loved to talk about my feelings. He subscribed to *Playboy*; I was a staunch feminist who decried the lack of women's roles in literature and film. He wasn't sure if he could ever marry a non-Jew; I was raised Catholic. We met in the swimming pool of our apartment complex. My skin was bronzed; his was so white, it was almost blue.

A year into our relationship, I got a job teaching in Yokohama, Japan. He didn't try to stop me, but he didn't want to break up with me, either. He thought that taking the job was a good idea, that I could use a cultural experience to broaden me.

After I lived in Yokohama for three months, he came to visit. Our reunion was fierce, sexy, a connection I craved even as it was happening. The next morning, when the sun was just sifting through my apartment's sliding-glass door, illuminating my Yokohama neighborhood, he reached for me.

But on our trip to Kyushu, he began hiding his head in pillows, not talking until the afternoon. I spent mornings in our hotel room, carefully writing in my journal, trying to mute the scratching of my pen.

Back from Japan with no job, no car, no money, I moved in with him. Not that no job, no car, and no money is an excuse. I loved him, in the way that … well, the way that a woman who isn't sure that she is loved loves.

Life can only be understood backward, but it must be lived forward, Søren Kierkegaard once said. I didn't know it at the time, but when I decided to take a poetry class, everything changed.

That was where I met Annie, the woman I woke up with in the hotel room, the woman who has been my lover, my life partner, for 13 years.

The first time we made love in that hotel bed, I turned over to sleep, and she said, "What are you doing?" She wanted us to hold each other, to talk a little, even. We drifted off to sleep midsentence, it seemed, and the next morning, when I awoke, I watched her in the blue light.

As though she could feel me watching her, she opened her eyes and said "Good morning." She smiled, even.

"Good morning," I replied. It had been so long since I'd spoken in the early morning. The words felt foreign in my mouth. I felt like a teenager doing something my parents had forbidden.

Funny that I'd feel that way about having *talked*, given that it was the first time I had *slept* with a woman. But sex with her, and sleeping with her, hadn't felt forbidden at all.

Now we often wake at dawn, just when the light is filtering into the bedroom. Annie pours us mugs of coffee and brings them back to bed. The dog snores on her dog pillow on the floor, and the cat squeezes into the crevice between our bodies. We lean back against the headboard and watch the unfolding light paint the room.

An artist and poet, Annie has taught me a few things about the dawn. Through the window, we observe the morning fog and the white house next door.

"Look at the white and gray beginning to brighten," she says. "Shadows are becoming more pronounced on the door. The sky is mixed with the same neutrals. Dawn makes neutrals. Even the green pine behind the house is a neutralized dark, cool gray."

We watch for a moment in silence. Then she tells me that, because of the fog, the gray, we'll see the sun open up from the top of the sky, rather than at the edge of the earth, the horizon. Gray, she says, is the color of waiting, the color of change.

GAMI

K'LEE WILLIAMS

Her hands touched my face, held my cheeks between her warm, papery smooth hands. The other people standing near were talking and laughing amongst themselves, seemingly unconcerned about the woman smoothing my curls from my forehead, gently cupping my chin in her hands, hugging me tightly to her ample, calico covered breasts.

This woman was my great-grandmother, my mother's grandmother, her father's mother.

I remember the tiny blue flowers of her dress, the clunky black shoes she wore, even the scent of the lily of the valley cologne she wore. My tiny fingers toyed with the lace collar on her dress. And, still she touched my face, her blind cataract clouded eyes almost silvery in color. She whispered silly songs about captains and maidens and whaling ships in my ear... and she smiled. Her smile made me feel happy inside, and I giggled loudly.

Everyone in the room, my mother and father, grandma and grandpa, and even all those other old people there in the visiting room of the nursing home laughed. Frightened by the noise, I hid my face in the woman's breasts, tightly pressed into her, the sweet scent and soft cloth covering her bosom comforting me.

For many minutes, perhaps hours, she rubbed my back, kissed my forehead, and shooed the 'others' away with a 'sshhhh! You are frightening the baby!'

I imagine it was my father who took me gently from her arms, carrying me to the car.
When later that afternoon, I woke from my nap confused, calling out "Gami, Gami, where Gami?" my father tried to soothe me with a silly song or two, and soon, I was again the happy toddler playing peek-a-boo with her daddy.
Gami died soon after our visit, or so I was told.

What I know for sure is that when I smell the sweet soft scent of lily of the valley cologne, I can feel Gami's hands touching my face and I can hear her soft voice telling me she loves me.

It is odd, really, the way so many adults create the aura of secrecy and sadness surrounding death. It could be their desire to protect the children. It could be their own fears. It could be many things, but what I believe is that whatever the reasons, this shrouded mystery and the loss that even young children often feel at the death or disappearance of someone they love is just a natural part of life.

Our society, in general, has seemingly odd rituals concerning death and memorialization of our loved ones. Sometimes, truly strange, at least in the eyes of young children, or maybe just in my eyes as a young child.

My other great-grandmother, mom's mom's mom, gosh, that was a mouthful, wasn't it? Anyway, Great Grandma had just three great grandchildren –

me, my cousin Karl and my cousin Brent. She had illusions about life that, even as a young girl, I thought were silly and strange.

She constantly interspersed French phrases with her everyday speech, although her family hadn't been in France since before Napolean Bonaparte. In fact, she'd been born in Rochester, New York, in 1865.

She would tell us the grand story of her grandfather, the hairdresser to Marie Antoinette on the fateful day she lost her head. He bundled his wife and children into a ragtag pony cart and they fled the burning city of Paris, running into the countryside to avoid the bloodthirsty and murderous crowds of hungry, apparently non-cake-eating revolutionary Parisians.

How did that happen? It didn't. When I grew old enough to delve into voluminous research at the library, I read everything I could get my hands on about the French Revolution, Marie Antoinette, Paris burning – basically, everything about my supposed family history. Fact is, most of what she told us was nothing more than her own affections with drama and her ability to 'stretch the truth'.

Regardless, we did love hearing her version of our family history. Or what we believed to be our family history.

Trey's Need

Kelsey Chasen

Trey and Alicia looked to be deep in conversation over in the quiet corner.

"Master, look at Alicia. She seems happy."

"So does Trey, sweetheart, so does Trey." Scott had often told Kyra he wanted his best friend to find the same kind of lifelong love that he had with her. It had been nearly four years since Amanda died. It was time for Trey to love again.

Trey had nursed Amanda through a long winter, when they had both believed she had some kind of bad cold—at first.

After several months of increasingly severe chest congestion, the fevers began in earnest. He had bundled her up finally and driven her into Seattle. University of Washington doctors had poked and prodded, done a multitude of CAT scans and MRIs, and still had no good news when they came to her room, solemnly.

Trey had stood by Amanda's bed, gripping her hand tightly while as the doctor explained that both her lungs were heavily spotted with numerous tumors, large and small.

"Cancer, Stage IV," they had said. Amanda had taken the news far better than her Master.

He had exploded. "Do something! Make her well!" he had screamed at the doctors.

"I am sorry, Mr. Greyson. There is nothing we can do. The cancer has metastasized."

"How long? How long does she have?" he'd begged.

"Months, at most, I'm afraid."

"Master, I want to go home, please?"

The doctors had tried to insist she remain in the hospital.

"Mr. Greyson, Ms. Alldridge, it would be best if you have the facilities of the hospice center here at the hospital, where you can be cared for properly." Trey hadn't even listened to them after that.

He took Amanda home.

Trey and Amanda were married the next evening, in their living room, with their friends all in attendance. Trey made them each promise him that there would be no tears but those of happiness.

After the ceremony, while Trey had been tucking his wife into their bed, they all made a vow, "To stand by them both, whatever comes."

They had all understood that Trey needed to take care of her, and they made schedules to help him with housework and shopping, bathing and feeding Amanda, whatever they needed, whenever they needed it.

The airplane manufacturing company where Trey worked was generous with family sick leave, but as the weeks wore on, Amanda getting weaker by the day, Trey confided to Scott that he was nearly out of leave, and concerned. Scott called their friends who also worked for the same company, and they managed to convince the company to let them pool their leave time, to allow Trey every minute possible with his wife.

The submissive coffee klatch group moved their weekly get-togethers to Amanda's bedside. For a few short hours on those Tuesday mornings, Trey would tend to the absolute necessities he couldn't avoid. The submissives cared for Amanda.

The girls in the group constantly had to remind each other of their vow to Trey, and it wasn't an easy task, holding the tears for their friend inside. When she had the energy, Amanda would talk to them about her dreams for Trey, once she was gone. She enlisted her friends in a campaign to take care of Trey...afterward.

After five weeks surrounded by her friends, and loved by Trey so tenderly, so completely, Amanda began to have more pain and some difficulty breathing. Trey called Dr. Lieberman.

"Doctor, this is Trey Greyson. Amanda needs pain medication. It has gotten almost nearly constant. Could you come out and take a look at her? It hurts her too much to bring her in to the office."

Dr. Lieberman arrived just three hours later. She brought a prescription bottle of quick-dissolve morphine tablets. She brought liquid morphine and syringes, for later. If he would allow hospice services, they would bring the oxygen compressor and set it up and train Amanda's caregivers.

"Trey, before we go in to see Amanda, I want to talk with you." They sat together on the sofa. "I need you to allow the hospice nurses to come out and train you on the equipment, and we will need to train a few of Amanda's friends to help you. We can set up the hospice training for tomorrow. They do still have their submissive coffee on Tuesdays, don't they?"

Trey nodded, tears trickling down his unshaven face. Dr. Lieberman patted Trey's hand. The two walked into the bedroom.

"Good morning, Dr. Lieberman. Good morning, Master," Amanda greeted them, trying to sit up in bed.

"No, love, you lay right there and rest."

Trey softly told his love he was going to help make her feel better, and tired as she was from the unceasing pain, she smiled at him. It did ease the pain. Trey held her closely, gently. After a few minutes, Amanda began to drift off and, a few moments later, she slept. They slipped out silently.

Scott and Alex were waiting for them in the living room. "Trey, the girls are worried about you. How can we help?" started Alex.

"Amanda wants to see her flower garden bloom from the window. She may not have enough time left to wait for full spring weather."

"Don't worry about the weather, Trey. She will see flowers from the window. The women will know how to make it happen," Alex said.

Scott could only nod, his heart breaking for his friend.

Dr. Lieberman gathered her things. She laid her hand on Trey's arm. "I'll have Hopeville Hospice give you a call about tomorrow. I will be back Thursday. You call me, Trey, any time, any time at all."

Trey rejoined his friends, sitting wearily on the couch. Scott watched his best friend but couldn't speak. Alex watched them both and didn't even try to speak. With a heavy sigh, Trey stood.

"I need to get back to Amanda, in case she wakes up. Thank you both for coming. It means the world to us both, the support."

Scott reminded Trey that Kyra and Beth would be at the house in a few minutes. "It's their turn to do laundry and make dinner, Trey, and I will be back tomorrow. You need to get out of the house, and I'll bring the horses. We will go for a ride while the submissive group is here with Amanda. The girls don't want us around then anyway. Then we can all be here for the hospice training."

On the short drive home, Scott called the community phone tree leader. "Helen, it's Scott. We need an emergency community meeting... Yes, about Trey and Amanda. Can you start the phone tree and see if we can't get it set up as soon as possible?... Sure, the pool house... Thank you, darlin'. Give me a call when you have the time set up."

That night, the entire community gathered in the pool house to work out their plan to help Trey and Amanda. Scott gently explained to the gathered group what they could do to help. Along with Amanda's wish to see masses of bright flowers in her garden was Trey's need for more help, physically and emotionally. His voice broke several times, his anguish evident on his face.

They formed instant committees, for companionship, housework and chores, even appointing Scott to act as Trey's liaison with not only the community itself, but also with Amanda's parents and family, estranged though they were.

The submissives would increase their visit schedule, giving Trey more time to spend with his slave without the worries of outside needs. The Dominants scheduled yard care and maintenance shifts.

The women drew up landscape plans and ordered hothouse plants by the cartload. They wanted to build Amanda huge raised beds so that she could see them easily from her bed. The men gathered tools and ordered lumber. John offered to take care of the couple's hair care and manicure needs. He would wash and condition Amanda's hair twice a week, more if she needed it. He would cut Trey's hair, too, right there at home. Now, all they needed was to find a massage therapist and perhaps someone with nursing experience for the last days.

The truckload of hothouse plants and flowers arrived that Friday afternoon. By nine in the morning on Saturday, thirty one people were pulling up the drive, trunks and the beds of the trucks loaded with plants and lumber, flowers and tools. By three that afternoon, all their friends quietly filed into their cars and left.

Trey lifted Amanda into his arms and sat on the edge of their bed. "Sweetheart, look at your gardens, your beautiful gardens."

She slowly turned her head to gaze out through the window, the pink glow of sunset shining through the foothills of the Cascades in the distance.

Her eyes sparkled from the Demerol, the garden surprise, or both. She weakly smiled.

"Master? I want to see closer. Please?" so Trey bundled her up in mounds of blankets and carried her out to the garden. She marveled at the myriad of colors and textures, all pinkened by the soft glow of sunset. He sat with her cradled in his arms while she enjoyed her gardens.

After a time, he tucked her safely back into bed.

She patted the coverlet, "Master, won't you please lay with me for a bit, until I fall asleep?"

Trey pulled off his heavy boots, shimmying out of his jeans. He slid in under the covers next to Amanda's thin body. Sliding his arm under her neck and holding her to him, they talked softly about the garden, their love, the end.

She told him, "I love you."

After a long moment, she took a strong breath, much stronger than she had in a long time. "Listen up, Master, you have to go on without me. Promise."

"I promise, my love. I promise."

Amanda died in his arms six weeks and four days later.

Scott drew Kyra into his arms. He could feel her remembering that time, that sad time, while she watched Trey with Alicia in the corner.

"I'm so glad he kept his promise, Master."

"Me too, my love." Scott let her stand there a moment lost in her memories before he said, "Darling, it is time for more surprises."

He kissed the top of the shining mass of hair flowing in waves down her back. Kyra looked up at her Master, gave him a small smile, wiped her tears on his shirt, and set about her duties.

I AM 30

NAMID

I am 30, and I walk with a cane. I am home-bound, and almost completely disabled. I do as much as I can with my work to help survivors of rape, incest, sexual abuse, sexual assault, and domestic violence, but there is another predator that has gotten the best of me.

I am 30, and I have MS: Multiple Sclerosis. My body has been battling this disease for over a decade, and due to many doctors' ignorance, my condition has worsened.

I am 30, and I have arthritis in every joint, including my spine. Have you ever had one of those days where your knee hurts, or your back hurts, or your hand hurts? Every day is like that for me, with one exception. Everything hurts. Both shoulders, both elbows, both hands, both hips, both knees, both ankles, my entire spine, even my jaw hurts. Every day is a battle with crippling arthritis and severe nerve pain. I have very limited mobility. I also have seizures, balance problems and other neurologic problems as a result of this disease.

I am 30, and my cane is a permanent fixture. "Eileen" (my cane, aptly named by my boss) has become my third leg. I can be found typically either in my bed or on the couch. I set up camp for the day, and do as much as my body will allow. I hobble around my house with Eileen for food and bathroom breaks. On a good day, I can make a few phone calls, answer some e-mails, and perhaps even write. On a bad day, I'm lucky to be awake for 6 hours.

I am 30, and although I am young, my body is old. It can be difficult to perform daily tasks, but there are worse things to battle in life.

I am 30, and my disease worsens by the day. I am on several medications, and am often being chauffeured to hospitals, doctors, or labs. It's not an ideal life for a 30 year old, but it'll do.

I am 30, and I have immersed myself in all things MS. I understand that this is a slowly progressing and fatal disease. This is my reality. I don't know how much more time I have on this planet. I could have a day, a year, a decade, or even a century. I simply do not know. I have come to terms with the fact that I need to get my will in order.

I write this, not for sympathy. You see, my life has been nothing but struggles and battles. That is what was destined for me by the powers above. Those struggles, trials and tribulations have given me great appreciation for life, and the people around me. The stars shine a little brighter. The scent of flowers is just a tad more pleasantly odiferous. Life is good.

I may be in a place that most 30 year olds will never face, but this is my life. Albeit painful and even frustrating at times, this is my life. I have no choice. So, I do the best that I can with each new day. I give out all the love that I can. I live my life as fully as possible.

I look back, and yes, I have made many mistakes. But I have no regrets. I have given myself some amazing opportunities. I have told the people in my life that I love them. I have done everything I could to the best of my ability. I immersed myself in every facet of life: art, music, dance, poetry and writing, science, history, math, linguistics, and more. I have loved many, and lost few. I have been blessed.

When I heard about *Arms Wide Open*, I originally felt that my story and "arms wide open" mentality were well shared in all my books. Then, something stirred in my heart. Suddenly, I felt I needed to tell my story – my story as an MS patient. To say that even with a crippling and debilitating disease, I continue to embrace my life with arms wide open.

I am 30, and although my time may be limited, my spirit is not. Regardless of whether I was sick or not, our end result is all the same. I may or may not survive this disease the way I have survived all of the other obstacles in my life, but regardless, I shall always call myself a survivor. That is my legacy.

Embrace your life, your passions, your people with arms wide open. You won't regret it, trust me.

SOMEONE FORMERLY KNOWN AS NOT-SO-BRAVEHEART

LEAH SAMUL

I don't consider myself to be a brave person. I avoid adventure and anything that might be risky, though I greatly admire those courageous souls who are daring and fearless. Firemen, policemen, emergency medical personnel and the like, fill me with grateful wonder; how can they do that stuff?

In quieter moments I often wonder why I am such an inveterate coward and security addict. I try to laugh about it. Remember the movie Braveheart, the story about the Scottish patriot William Wallace? I'm a Not-So-Braveheart. Instead of "Dances-With-Wolves," the poetic name Native Americans gave to Kevin Costner's character in the eponymous movie, my name would be something like "Afraid-Of-Her-Own-Shadow." I make jokes about this to my friends, because seriously thinking about my life-long, hair-trigger anxiety depresses me.

One night, I think it was in 1978, I was coming home at around 9:00 p.m. on a Friday evening. I lived with two roommates in San Francisco's upscale Nob Hill. The next day, the three of us would be moving to a cheaper and quieter house out on the avenues near the ocean. After work, we had met downtown to celebrate the move, but I was tired and left a little early. I don't remember where we were celebrating, but it was close enough for me to walk back to our soon-to-be former apartment. When I was a few blocks from our flat, I heard noise coming from the underground parking structure of a swank apartment complex. The parking garage was wide open and though I was on the opposite side of the street, I could see what was causing the commotion. A tall and muscled man was forcibly pulling a young woman into a car, against her will. A substantial collection of gold chains hung from the man's neck; he wore the open shirt and bell-bottoms that were typical of the '70s.

You have to feature this scene: about 10 people, both men and women, all of them elegantly attired in long gowns and tuxedos, were standing around and watching this abduction. The woman being pulled into the car had on green pants and a pullover top. She was all of five feet tall, and she was barefoot. She kept yelling at the guy, "no, I'm not going with you!" She was reaching out to hold on to the parking garage railing. He was angry, calling her a stupid bitch and using other choice terms to tell her what he thought of her.

No one was making a move to help her.

I remembered the famous incident that occurred in New York City a number of years back.

A woman was stabbed to death on the street, and though many people saw it—something like 40 or 50—no one came to help. I was born upstate, in Buffalo, and at the time I heard the story I told myself it would never have happened in my home town. In Buffalo, someone would have come forward. So there I was, a transplanted upstate New Yorker, living in a city I loved, watching this ugly spectacle.

"What happened in New York City was different, " I told myself. "This is probably a pimp and his hooker; don't get involved, it's not your business and besides, the guy obviously works out. How could you possibly do anything? You'll create more of a mess. Don't be a do-gooder. Just walk on."

But, I thought, even if she is a hooker, she's getting mistreated. That's not right. Besides, if I were being dragged into a car against my will, wouldn't I want someone to at least call the cops? And I'm a feminist. Aren't we women supposed to help each other? "Yes," I answered myself, "on both counts."

As the two continued to struggle, and with my pulse at aerobic level, I walked to the phone booth that was in the garage. I got close to the guy, and said (it must have seemed totally lame) "Excuse me sir." When he turned to me, I got my face level with her face, looked right in her eyes, and asked "Do you want the cops called?" She responded affirmatively. For a moment, the man stared at me in complete disbelief. Then he yanked really hard and wrenched her away, carrying her to his car as she fought to get free. He threw her into the passenger's side with enormous force, and as I called the police, I thought she'd hit her head on the steering wheel.

With an arrogant, almost casual saunter, he walked to the driver's side, but she had astoundingly bolted and was again running back to the railing to hang on. All the while, the crowd of people still watched. No one came close to me to offer any protection or to stand near me in support, though they had to see I was trying to help. I had dialed 911 and was told that the police were on their way, but I was feeling more insecure by the moment. This was Friday night, and I assumed the cops were busy with crimes of weapons and drugs.

By the time I hung up, she had reached the railing. "The cops are coming." I said loudly, trying to sound confident. I was so scared I felt like I was having an out of the body experience, but I went over and stood by her on the railing. The guy paused, and then got into the car. I was thrilled; he's leaving.

"Looks like he's going," I said happily as we stood there.

"No, he's not going anywhere," she said. "When he threw me in the car, I got his keys."

If she was a hooker, she was a smart one. I saw him looking for the keys on the floor, and then he realized what had happened.

He walked back to us. No more profanity this time. Now he spoke with honeyed tones. "Oh, come on, sweetie, we can take care of this. It's going to be okay; we can just go. Let's just get out of here. Come on, sweetie . . ."

And then, miracle of miracles, the police arrived. They must have had squad cars patrolling area, because it took them less than a minute to get to us.

As they walked in, I went toward them and said, "There's the woman who needs your help." Then I left, without giving them my name, and walked the two blocks home as fast as I could. I was still scared, and it took me several hours to fall asleep.

I never asked her name. I thought I heard him call her Debbie or Denise or something like that, but I'm not sure. I have no idea what happened to her. Hooker or not, I hope she's okay and that she could get free from the violence she experienced that night. And I hope the guy learned something, too. If you perpetrate violence you have to be prepared to accept the consequences. Someone formerly known as a Not-So-Braveheart might be watching, and just might be able to summon up the courage to call the cops.

GOOD-BYE, EMILY DICKINSON

SMOKY TRUDEAU

Why is it that while they're alive, great artists seem to get more attention for being crazy than for being talented? Just look at Vincent van Gogh. His peers referred to him as the Fou Roux, or the red-headed madman, and he became famous—or rather, infamous—for trying to attack Paul Gaugin with an open razor when they got into a dispute. Gaugin stopped Vincent, but van Gogh somehow managed to cut a slice off his own ear in the process. He ended up in a lunatic asylum. By the time the poor guy died at the ripe old age of 37, he had sold only one painting, The Red Vineyard, to one Miss Ann Boch for a paltry four hundred francs. That's only about eighty dollars. Not a fortune, even by 1890 standards. Then he up and died a few months later. Nowadays more grade school kids know of van Gogh because he cut off his ear, not because he painted Starry Night.

Or, how about Sylvia Plath? Everyone knows she committed suicide by sticking her head in the oven and turning on the gas. If that's not crazy, I don't know what is. But how many people can list the names of, say, five of her poems? Sylvia was just 31 when she died.

There's also my favorite jazz musician, Charlie "Bird" Parker. I reckon he got famous enough during his lifetime, and he opened the famous Birdland Jazz Club in New York and all that, but his fame was overshadowed by his multiple suicide attempts and hospitalizations. Charlie died from heart failure and cirrhosis of the liver, diseases more common in men in their sixties than Charlie's 34 years.

And then there's Emily Dickinson. She's probably the finest poet the world has ever seen, excepting maybe Shakespeare. Shakespeare wasn't considered crazy, but there's been a big debate recently over whether he really was the author of all the stuff credited to him. There are people who think Frances Bacon, or Christopher Marlowe, or, shoot, even Queen Elizabeth the First actually wrote his stuff. That would make Shakespeare a thief, but not necessarily crazy.

Emily wasn't an angry crazy, like van Gogh, or a suicidal crazy, like Charlie Parker or Sylvia Plath. No, Emily was considered a nutcase because she was a strange duck, an introvert who rarely left her home. Toward the end of her life, she barely made it out of her bedroom. It wasn't until after her death that her sister Lavinia found her extensive collection of poems. Lavinia had them published, ironically, in 1890, the same year Vincent van Gogh died. At least Emily outlived Vincent, Sylvia, and Charlie. She was 55 when she died. Heck, she even outlived that thief Shakespeare. He only made it to 52.

I have no opinion on Charlie's premature death or Sylvia's suicide, other than that they were tragedies. I don't care much if Shakespeare was a thief, or about Vincent dying broke. I mean, that was a tough break for him and all, but it really didn't have anything much to do with me. I don't even care if people thought they all were crazy, although if anyone asked me I'd say the whole world is crazy if you have to be dead to be appreciated.

But Emily—Emily is a different story. I care what people say about her. Emily has everything to do with me.

ଷଷଷ

August is always hot around here, but this year it has sizzled like Hades. The temperature has hit one hundred degrees eleven days in a row, and it doesn't cool off much below ninety at night. I can't believe there are still idiots out there who think global warming is a plot made up by the tree-huggers and the nature worshippers. All you need to do is stand outside for five minutes on a day like today and you know something isn't right with the climate.

The heat is taking its toll on everybody. I read in a newspaper that a man shot his wife because their air conditioner blew up when she turned on the blender and overloaded their electrical circuits. The rats that live in the pedestrian tunnel under the railroad tracks stumble around looking half drunk. Birds fly in slow motion, like they're flying through Jell-o.

The heat has left me feeling none too good myself, but I have to work for a living. How happy is the little stone/ that rambles in the road alone/ and doesn't care about careers/ and exigencies never fears. Yeah, right. That attitude might have been all right for old Emily and for stones, but it doesn't work for me. I don't have the luxury of being able to stay home even when I feel under the weather. So, on day twelve of the heat wave, I get dressed in my finest red lace bustier (even if I am well past sixty, I can still turn heads in a bustier, just like that singer—you know, that Madonna lady), the pink feather boa I found in the dumpster outside the Tivoli theater over on Second Street, my favorite sky-blue polyester pants, and pink mules I found along with the boa. Being an artist, I have an image to maintain. I duck out my front door, take my wheels from the garage and, popping a wheelie, head for work.

ক্ষক্ষক্ষ

This isn't the way things always were. I went to college, got a teaching degree. Met a man, Walter. Got married. Taught school. Normal stuff. The best times were those spent at the beach, when Sam, Jeremy and Ella were little. God never blessed Walter and me with a child of our own; those three little rascals belonged to his sister Delores, but I loved them like they were mine. We took them to the Outer Banks one summer while their parents went to Africa on a month-long work project with the church. I read to them while we sunned ourselves on the beach: the poetry of Sylvia Plath, the short stories of Ernest Hemmingway, Moby Dick.

And Emily Dickinson. Most of all, I loved to read Emily Dickinson to them. Or sing it. Sometimes, I sang.

"Did you know, Ella, that you can sing almost all Emily Dickinson's poems to the tune of The Yellow Rose of Texas?" I asked one day as we sat on the porch of our rented beachside cottage.

It was raining that day, and the water broke along the beach in angry whitecaps. Ella was grouchy and in a petulant mood. She loved the beach. I knew she wanted to splash at the water's edge, look for sand dollars and starfish and shark teeth. She wanted Uncle Walter to throw her off his shoulders in the water, and me to bury her in sand. These are the things a perfect day at the beach are made of when you're a child.

She didn't answer me, so I broke out in song.
"Two butterflies went out at noon
And waltzed above a stream,
Then stepped straight through the firmament
And rested on a beam;"

I looked at her, but she wasn't budging. She was glum, remember? I kept singing.
"And then together bore away
Upon the shining sea,—
Though never yet, in any port,
Their coming mentioned be."

She giggled. I was encouraged, and being nothing if not persistent, I finished the poem:

"If spoken by the distant bird,
If met in ether sea

By frigate or by merchantman,
Report was not to me."

It was too much for her. She burst out into a combination squeal and belly laugh, a sound only a ten-year-old girl is physically capable of making.

"See, what did I tell you? The Yellow Rose of Texas. Works just about every time."

"Sing another one," she begged.

I did. And another, and another after that. Every single poem I picked could be sung to the tune of The Yellow Rose of Texas.

Once I got curious to know if Dickinson wrote her poems that way on purpose. I found out the song was written during her lifetime, in 1853, but it really didn't get popular until more than a hundred years later when Mitch Miller recorded it. Somehow, I doubt it was intentional. I mean, Yellow Rose of Texas isn't exactly the prettiest song ever written, you know what I mean? Emily Dickinson was feminine and refined. She'd probably have set her songs to something much more proper, like a ballad or a love song.

ॐॐॐ

The big clock outside the train station reads 8:53 a.m. How can it be so damned hot this early in the morning, I wonder. The wheels of my shopping cart make a dull, thwapping sound, and keep getting stuck in patches of sticky asphalt. I think again about working at home, where it is a bit cooler in the protective shade of the railway overpass. But people expect me to be at work. I keep going. Thwap, thwap goes the cart.

"Ninety-three degrees."   My nephew Sam wipes a spot of grease from his face with a sad excuse for a handkerchief as he walks out of the Sinclair service station and hands me an icy cold Dr. Pepper. "Ninety-four, tops." Sam runs the only gas station in town that still pumps gas and checks under the hood for its customers.

Together, we check the temperature on the thermometer next to the gas pumps. This is our daily ritual. The little red line falls right at the ninety-three degree line.

Sam grins. "Am I good or what? Channel Six should hire me as a weather bunny."

"You'd be one ugly weather bunny." I take a swig from my Dr. Pepper, then rub the cold bottle over the back of my neck, savoring the chill it sends down my spine. "I think you cheat and look before I get here."

"If you'd let me fix that flat tire for you, I'd have to look.   As it is, I can tell what the temperature is when you're a block away just by the sound that thing makes on the pavement."

"No point in fixing it.   It'll just go flat again." I put the empty Dr. Pepper bottle in the bottle return rack by the door.   Truth be told, I wouldn't mind him fixing my tire. It would make the cart a lot easier to push. But that would ruin our little game, so Sam continues to ask, and I continue to decline. "Thanks for the drink." I head down the sidewalk once again.

"See ya tomorrow, Miss Dickinson," Sam calls.

Sam is a truly kind individual. Once when he was a little boy he found a baby robin that had fallen out of the nest. The nest was too high up in the tree for Sam to put the baby back, so he took it home and fed it minced cat food and sugar water until it got big enough to survive on its own. *If I shouldn't be alive when the robins come/ give the one in red cravat a memorial crumb.* Old Emily would have been proud of Sam. He not only gave that baby bird a crumb, he gave it the whole loaf.

The bus stop on the corner of Main and Second is one of my favorite places to work. It has a nice bench for me to sit on and a good place to park my cart while I write. Besides, there's a lot of action downtown, and it inspires me. I can spend hours sitting on that bench, watching the people come and go and writing my poems. Usually, no one bothers me much, and occasionally someone gives me a dollar or two, even if I didn't ask for it. I work hard to earn my living. People know that, and pay me accordingly.

I haven't always been a poet. I didn't write my first poem until I was fifty-five years old. But great art knows no boundaries when it comes to age. Grandma Moses didn't create her first painting until she was seventy-six. I figure that gives me a twenty-one year edge over her.

ॐॐॐ

I sit at the bus stop for two hours, looking and watching and writing. It's a good morning, and I get twenty-three pages of poetry written. Old Emily herself couldn't have done better. But then my pen runs out of ink. I rummage around in my cart, but I can't find another one, so I put my notebook away.

I keep my notebooks sorted by color and size, with the oldest ones on the bottom and the new ones on top. Red, yellow, blue, green, black, red, yellow, blue, green, black. One time, I found a notebook that was orange. I kept it for a while, but there was no room for an orange pile in my cart, so I ended up throwing it back in the dumpster.

Since I can't write anymore I decide to go to the park and give a reading. I'm getting awfully hot, but like I already said, people expect me at work.

There's a big granite rock at the edge of the park engraved with the names of the forty-two men from town who have died defending our country—more proof that greatness is not appreciated until after a person is dead.

My husband's name is number forty-one on the list. Walter E. Jorgens, Private First Class. Walter died in Viet Nam when some drunken fool from his own platoon tossed a grenade at the privy. Walter died with his pants down, two days before the war ended and his unit returned home.

I held my head high like a grieving widow should. But I saw how people snickered and whispered behind my back about Walter's embarrassing demise. That nearly killed me, being laughed at like that. Before Walter died, I was a respected citizen in this town. In the years following his death, I became a pariah. I had to quit my job—I taught freshman literature at the high school—because my students would look at me like I was speaking in tongues while standing naked in front of them. I knew what they were thinking. They were thinking what a fool I must have been, being married to a guy who got himself blown up in a privy.

I complained to the principal, and he sat in on a few of my classes. He said he didn't see what my problem was. That's when I realized he, too, took me for a fool. I quit on the spot.

I run my fingers over Walter's name, like I do every time I come to the rock. *I reason that in heaven somehow/ it will be even...* I wonder what tragedy inspired old Emily to write such words.

Next to the memorial is a sign that reads "Exercise Your First Amendment Rights Here." That's where I stand to do my readings. I consider it a public service to share my art with my fellow citizens.

I tie a box labeled "Payment for Services Rendered" to the front of my cart. People may laugh and whisper about me behind my back, but at least they pay me for my work. I think they do it out of guilt, but as old Emily said, *Remorse is cureless/ the disease not even God can heal.*

I choose a poem from the ones I wrote at the bus stop and begin reading.

"And the bus rolled up—loud, smelly,
and the businessmen poured out—poured out
like coins from a slot machine
when you hit the jackpot.
And the businessmen all carry
briefcases and newspapers,
and don't see the beauty of the world around them,
And I praise God!
Praise God that I don't have a briefcase,
and I can see the beauty of the world."

A woman in sneakers and a linen business suit dashes past, throwing me a look I don't like, an

"I'm better-than-you" kind of look. But she tossed three quarters in my payment box, so maybe she was just hot. I make two dollars and forty-seven cents that morning.

Getting hungry, I pocket my pay and head over to the First Presbyterian Church for a sandwich and, I hope, a glass of sweet tea to cool me off. First Presby serves lunch Tuesdays, Wednesdays, and Fridays. I try hard not to miss out on lunch those days because the rest of the week I have to fend for myself. I used to go to the soup kitchen at the Congregational church across town for lunch on Mondays and Thursdays, but they had too many steps and I always had to leave my cart outside. One day, I came out and found a bunch of teenaged goons ripping up my notebooks and throwing them all over the parking lot.

"Hey Poet, this is what we think of your stuff, you crazy old hag," they jeered before running off. Cowards. I lost twenty-one notebooks that day. I still grieve deeply.

I like First Presby. They have a wheelchair ramp leading into the building, and the pastor lets me take my cart inside.

I get half a bologna-and-cheese sandwich, some potato chips, two carrot sticks, and praise Jesus, my glass of sweet tea. I take a seat by Reverend Jeremy—yes, my other nephew is a preacher—who is sitting at a table with a scruffy-looking wino.

"Emily! How good to see you." Jeremy, like Sam, always calls me by my right name. I appreciate that.

"Hey, Poet, talked to your mother recently?" the wino asks through a mouthful of potato chips.

"All morning long. Who've you been talking to, Bill? The bottom of a Strawberry Hill bottle?"

"Ain't none of your business. But since you asked, I spent the day with Billy Shakespeare. He's my dad, ya know." He throws his head back and laughs as if he has just told the funniest joke in the world. A piece of carrot stuck in the gap between the two yellow teeth he has left in the front of his mouth gives him the look of a Halloween jack-o-lantern past its prime. Stumbling slightly, he gets up from the table and slaps the reverend on the back. "See ya, Rev." He lurches out into the hot sunshine, still laughing.

I shake my head and turn back to my sandwich. "He's just jealous because I come from a famous family," I say.

Jeremy gives me a cow-eyed smile that, from anyone else, I would take as pity. I don't take kindly to people pitying me, like they think I'm crazy or something just because I'm Emily Dickinson's daughter.

"But Emily Dickinson never married—she never had any children," the pity-givers say. "She was a recluse." Or, they say, "How can you be Emily Dickinson's daughter? She died a hundred years ago. She couldn't have a daughter your age." I just look at them. I don't have to explain myself to the pity-givers.

"I picked up a few things for you," he says, pushing a manila envelope across the table to me.

I open the envelope. Inside are two black pens with "Edwards Funeral Home and Mortuary" written on the sides, a green, college-ruled notebook that looks like it has never been used, and three boxes of matches engraved with the words, "Hillary and Brian, July 26, 1998."

That's another thing I like about First Presby. Like his brother Sam, Reverend Jeremy does me these kindnesses. I thank him before getting up to leave.

"Why don't you stay in here where it's cool to work this afternoon, Emily?" he asks.

"Oh sacrament of summer days/ oh, last communion in the haze..." I grin at the reverend. "You wouldn't deny me the privilege of partaking in the sacrament of this glorious, hazy summer day now, would you Reverend? I'd think you'd know all about the importance of sacraments."

"I don't think old Emily was referring to city smog when she wrote that poem. There's a heat advisory today. It's dangerous for you to be out there."

"Thanks, but no. You know I don't like to be cooped up inside." I adjust my feather boa, grab my cart, and leave before he can protest too much.

That's the one thing that irks me about the reverend—he's always trying to get me to do things I don't want to do. A few years back—it was right after he graduated from seminary, all full of delusions about the meaning of Christian charity—he took me to the doctor for a check-up. I hadn't seen a doctor in ten years, so I figured what could it hurt?

The doctor gave me these pills he said would make people stop laughing and whispering behind my back. I didn't see how my swallowing a pill could affect how someone else behaved, but I gave them a try if only to make the reverend happy.

Those pills made me feel as dull as a six-month old razor. I couldn't think clearly. I couldn't write my poetry. I threw the pills in the trash.

Well, that upset the reverend pretty bad. He went to court and tried to have me committed to some mental hospital so that I'd have to take my medicine. But the judge wouldn't do it. He told the reverend only a blood relative or a legal guardian could have me committed. Since the reverend was my nephew by marriage, not by blood, I was free to take or not take my medicine so long as I wasn't a threat to myself or anybody else. I liked that judge a whole lot more than I liked the reverend that day.

Another time, he and Sam took me downtown to one of those dumpy little hotels where they cram you in like sardines. An SRO, Sam said it was called. He and Jeremy hadn't been happy when I moved into my current home. Not that I'd had much of a choice—Walter's life insurance paid off the mortgage on our little house, and I had some savings, but even though I'm a frugal person the money eventually ran out. When the city threatened to condemn the house because it needed a new roof and foundation repairs, Sam and the reverend both offered to take me in. But no way was I going to move in with either of them. I've got my pride—I can take care of myself. Anyway, I took one look at that SRO with its pee-stained walls and told them no thanks. I liked my place just fine.

And why wouldn't I? I have the nicest place along the tracks. I am the proud owner of a two-box domicile; one room for sleeping and one for when

I'm awake, compliments of a local moving company. On the outside I drew a picture of a flowerbox full of yellow daffodils, using some permanent markers I found in an Oscar the Grouch backpack some kid had left at the bus stop by mistake. I drew daffodils in honor of old Emily. She must have liked daffodils a lot, because she mentioned them in quite a few of her poems. The daffodils make my place pretty, and they keep Bill and a couple of my other neighbors from trying to steal it while I'm at work. None of them are artists; they don't appreciate things like daffodils.

I do love art. I don't have much use for that weird modern art—When Sam and Jeremy and Ella were just toddlers they could paint as well as that Jackson Pollack did in his prime. I don't care for cubism, modernism, futurism, surrealism, or any of those other "isms." But I love the French impressionists. I love Monet, Manet, Degas. I love Gauguin and Pissarro. But most of all, I love Vincent van Gogh.

That's why I painted window boxes on my place. Vincent van Gogh wouldn't have lived in a house that didn't have window boxes and flowers. I refuse to either.

Daffodils aside, the best part about my place is the garage for my wheels. That garage was a lucky find. It said "Frigidaire" on the side, but since I found it in the ditch next to the tracks, I figured old Mr. Frigid Aire didn't need it any more. It keeps my notebooks nice and dry when rain leaks down from the overpass.

I sit on the stairs of the public library for a while, and write eight more poems, but the librarian comes out and tells me to move on. I haven't been welcome at the library since the time six months ago that I tried to sneak out under my sweater a copy of The Poems of Emily Dickinson. I wasn't trying to steal it. Just borrow it. I told the librarian I wasn't allowed to renew my library card after I lost my house because I didn't have a permanent address. The librarian was unsympathetic, and barred me from using the library.

You'd think a librarian would know better than to dismiss an important literary figure like I am destined to become. But no. Like I said before, great artists never get the respect they deserve while they are alive. I move on.

I try to give another reading outside the post office, but a policeman tells me I can't do that either—that I am preventing people from conducting official U.S. Post Office business by blocking the door. I'm pretty tired, very hot, and feeling poorly. I think maybe the bologna in my sandwich had gone bad. Anyway, I decide to go home.

The Sinclair station is closed when I pass it on my way home, so I can't get another free pop from Sam. I decide maybe I'll buy one from the pop machine anyway, but when I reach in the pocket of my pants to get some of my earnings from the poetry reading in the park, I find I've lost most of it through a hole I didn't know was there. By the time I get home, I just want to lie down, I'm so dizzy from the heat.

I park my cart in the garage, take my new notebook and one of the new pens, and crawl into my bedroom to rest. I try to write, but I'm too hot and thirsty. I have a splitting headache, and I can't concentrate. I think, maybe I'll go up to the train station and get me some water from the fountain. But that would mean moving, and I'm tired. I don't want to get up.

I hear her before I see her. *"'That others could exist while she must finish quite/ a jealousy for her arose so nearly infinite.'"*

And then I see her. Emily Dickinson, a vision in white, coming towards me from the dark underpass. She is smiling at me.

"Great artists never get the respect they deserve while they are alive," she says, and reaches out to take my hand.

I think about staying. Sam, and Jeremy and Ella will miss me if I go. What will happen to my notebooks?

But Emily is leaving now, heading back down the underpass.

I shut my notebook and follow.

Forest Song Little Mother

Vila SpiderHawk

Chapter Nine

"You must really miss your children," Gerda smoothed the green cotton my mother had brought the night before. Matka Lasu laid the pattern for the pants on the cloth and smiled around a mouthful of pins. She plucked the pins from her mouth and clumped them on the kitchen table.

"Oh no. I'm with them every day."

Gerda managed to produce a nondescript smile.

"Matka Lasu means mother of the woods, *liebchen*. I am mother to everything you see."

"So you never had children?"

"Oh yes, more than I can count." She stuck a pin into the pattern then searched the young woman's eyes. "You miss her terribly."

"Yes, we were very close." She clicked her thumbnails together, a habit she'd adopted since they'd reached her fingertips. I found it slightly annoying.

"I think you need a manicure," I suggested from the sink. I dried the last of the dishes and put them away, trying not to hear the clicking.

"It's hard when you don't have a chance to say goodbye." My teacher poked the rest of the pins into the cloth and Gerda penciled the dots for the pleats. "We could have a memorial if you'd like."

"What I really want is Mama alive." Gerda tugged at the paisley babushka she'd worn since my mother had brought it three weeks before.

Suddenly I feared losing Matka Lasu. She'd grown old since the war had begun. She pressed her hand to the cloth, and ridges grew like a grove from the web between her pointer and thumb. The creases of her smile lingered when the smile was gone, and a slender streak of white had striped her hair. Not wanting to imagine how I'd get along without her, I bit my thumb and forgave Gerda's clicking.

"Here, I'll cut," I atoned, picking up the shears. Matka Lasu reclaimed the straight pins as I cut and, removing the pattern, pinned pant panels together. Gerda sniffled and threaded a needle. I was ashamed of my joy that I wouldn't have to sew.

"You'll never guess what!" Bożena, in a yellow sundress, her blonde hair a halo of curls, bounded into the house, a young man in tow. I'd grown used to her in pants. She looked odd in a dress, and yet she glowed with the excitement of love. His cheeks were hollow and smooth, and his wiry brown hair was just a little too long. His eyes were sullen and dark. I knew I'd seen him before, but I couldn't fix a name to the face. She saw Gerda and stopped and squeaked a little chirp when the young man stumbled into her. "I'm so sorry. I didn't know you had a guest. I'm Bożena." She thrust her hand at Gerda. "And this is Gerhard! You remember Gerhard, don't you, Judy?" I nodded, though to me he was a stranger. Tugging her babushka, Gerda shook the woman's hand. "You met him at the Seder." We had had many Seders. "The first year! You couldn't possibly forget!"

"You gave me a choice of going to Sweden or staying in this Godforsaken place." A sheepish grin curled his lips so charmingly that I saw why Bożena loved him so. She threw her arms around his waist, contentment glowing from her pores. "But I discovered another option. Bożena's family invited me to move in with them, and I joined them in the underground."

"And now we're going to have a baby!" She clapped a hand to her giggle. My teacher shot across the room and swathed them both in a hug. "Where's Tranoc? I'd really hoped to tell you all."

"He's with the fairies. They're preparing for another run tonight." My embrace lacked Matka Lasu's zeal. "Do you think this is a good time to have a child?" I slapped my hand to my mouth but the words had tumbled out. They hung like a foul odor at a wedding.

"Well this wasn't a choice that we consciously made." I hated that I'd made her defensive.

"What better time to celebrate new life than during war?" Gerda stood and shook the couple's hands. "Congratulations, you two. However ugly things get you will have a beautiful child."

"Gerda's right. Oh! I'm sorry! This is Gerda. Gerda Felden. She's a friend of my mother's and a dear friend of mine. May I touch?" I reached out to examine the child. "Do you want to know the baby's sex?" Nodding, she smiled the kind of forgiveness that only a mother can give. She placed my hands to her flat belly, and I closed my eyes. In the image that flashed, Bożena clutched the little girl and wailed her lover's name to the hills. I swallowed my fear. "Your daughter will be blonde."

"Will she be healthy?" Her eyes mirrored my dread.

"Oh yes!" I worked too hard to stitch a smile to my face. "Your daughter is going to be fine." I glanced at Matka Lasu. She had seen the vision too. Her eyes were just recovering from gray.

"Let's bless this child and the parents who made her," she suggested with a grin that was too broad. But the herbs she chose were for protection, not for blessing. "Sit here," she instructed, folding up the sewing project and placing it on a wingback chair. She spread two squares of red cloth about the size of my hand on the table and drew *kura stopa* on each.

"Hen's feet?" Bożena squinted at my teacher then at me. "The *znak* of protection? Why?"

"Hen's feet are the symbol of motherly protection. What else would you draw for a child?" But I knew Matka Lasu was drawing the defense that only a Goddess could provide. She sprinkled hyssop and marigold onto the squares. "Put your hands on the cloths," she directed. Leaning on his elbows, Gerhard folded his hands and rested his chin on them. Bożena pleaded with her eyes and stroked her belly. Sighing with elaborate self-control, he laid his fingers on the cloths next to hers. My teacher lit a black candle and, whispering a spell, walked three times counter clockwise around them. She placed the candle on the table and lit a red one. "Do the blessing, Kochanie. I'll be right behind you." Not knowing what to say, I bit my nail then spoke, trusting that the right words would come out.

"The Zorya protect you both day and night with their shimmering silvery light. Whatever the danger, whatever the fright, they defend you with all their might." Going clockwise, I circled the couple three times then set my candle next to my teacher's.

"As we say it, so it is," my teacher clapped three times.

"So it is," I repeated and clapped my hands too. She threaded two needles with red thread.

"Let's make *ladanki* of these." She gave a needle to me. "Wear these sachets every moment of the day and night, even when you bathe or sleep," she commanded as she whip-stitched two edges together. "Do you have some red ribbon?" I still had some from the party to celebrate the first dress I had made. I brought two lengths to the table. My teacher laid one on her cloth and sewed the final side around it. She tied the ribbon with three knots and hung the necklace on Gerhard. I did the same with mine for Bożena. "Now let's go have a picnic! We have a life to celebrate!" Bożena glanced at her watch and winced.

"I'm so sorry. There's no time. Do you have the passport paper?"

"At the house." My teacher smiled an apology to Gerda. "I have to go. Will you two be all right?" We assured her that we would, though I knew I'd have to sew. I had kissed them goodbye and had seen them out the door before remembering Gerda's nails.

"Oh, Bożena! Could you bring some manicure stuff for Gerda the next time you come? And maybe a lipstick," I added in a whisper, hoping to make it a surprise.

"I'll send it with Pani Pohronezny tonight or with Bodgan or whoever comes." She kissed me on both cheeks and then nudged Gerhard forward. He bowed from the waist and kissed my hand.

"Good to see you again." He curled a finger in the ribbon, and I knew he'd tear the talisman from his neck before he'd reached the edge of the woods. I cast an extra shield of light, and it rested on his body but then gusted away on September's gentle breath.

"You can't change a person's fate," I thought I'd said silently.

"I'm sorry, what?" Gerda peeked from the wingback.

"These trousers can wait. Let's go for a walk. In fact let's have that picnic Matka Lasu talked about." Snatching up the quilt and the gathering basket, I yanked her through the door before she had a chance to voice her predictable protestations. Gerda hated the woods. Nonetheless I nursed a hope that once she got to know them, she would love them.

She picked her way through the brush as if at any moment a monster would appear to eat her up. To distract her I pointed out the heather in a clearing. "*Wrzesień* is the Polish word for September, and it comes from *wrzosiec*, the Polish word for heather." She smiled politely but defensively waved her arms as if she were a blind woman. "An infusion of the flowers can calm nervousness, help you sleep, and ease the pain of rheumatism." She snapped a twig with a step and, gasping, jerked her head. Her hand flew to her heart. She stood rock still. I was sorry I had brought her. She had been through enough. "Let's go back," I suggested. She gawked over my head. Her panic seized me by the throat. I spun around and, clapping, laughed.

Stretched to his full height, Rościsław hulked, as he'd done from time to time since, as the runt, he'd outgrown his litter mate, Czarownica. I hadn't seen the bear all summer. I launched myself into his chest then grabbed for Gerda so she would not run away. There was no need. She couldn't move. "Oh Rościsław's a good friend, unless you make a move to harm me." He laid his front paws on my shoulders and brushed my face with his. I kissed his cheek and he went back down on all fours. He nudged my chest. I understood that he was trying to tell me something but Gerda's fear interfered with the telepathy. He looked back over his shoulder then nudged my chest again.

Wound! Frustration sharpened the word.

"Is somebody hurt?" As stressed animals do, he grunted and shifted his weight from side to side. I turned to Gerda. "Do you think you can find your way home?" Eyes wide, she shook her head and clung like worry to my hand. "I have to go, and there's no time. I'm going to take you back to my place the way Heidi brought you out of the camp." I wrapped my arms around her waist and concentrated on the char mark in the floor just in front of the hearth. We landed just outside the door. "I'm sorry," I said, giving thanks that at least we hadn't landed in the sink. "But I have to leave."

"I'll be here." Heidi called and opened the door. I was gone before Gerda was inside. This time I landed where I'd planned— just in front of the bear. Gripping fistfuls of his hair, I leapt to his back and rode.

Lumbering through hazels and lindens and yews, past white willows and walnuts, and pines, the trees strewing sunlight petals in our path, the floral taste in full fortissimo, I spurred him brutally forward, urging him to speeds he was simply not able to maintain.

We found the man on his belly near an elderberry bush. I leapt from Rościsław's back and, dropping to my knees, did a quick assessment of the man's condition. His shirt was torn. A shoe was missing. Though I didn't see blood, a knot the size of a walnut had risen from the edge of his ginger colored curls. I rolled him over. He groaned.

"Oh Klaus!" My moan towed with it the memory of the shy blue-eyed young man who'd delivered new oxfords through the bars of my father's fence. I saw his image again as his spirit had appeared the second time on the night of my woman ritual. Dressed in white, a wheat head wreath glinting in the full moon's light, he'd had the poise and the beauty of a god. Matka Lasu had proclaimed that he would be my true love, the Jarilo to my Dzydzilelya. The man of the moment had blackened eyes. His ear was swollen. Dried blood streaked across his cheek and still dribbled from each of his nostrils.

This was not what I'd expected. I had wished for my lover to ride in on a steed looking golden and handsome and strong. I had hoped for a champion who would cherish and protect me, not a broken, bleeding man in need of care. I'd wanted flowers, and charm, maybe even poetry. And I'd wanted to feel the kind of glowing adoration that had glistened in Bożena's eyes. So absorbed was I in my romantic disappointment that I almost missed the rustling in the woods.

"He's just a Jew." The words, clipped to precise sharp angled bits, startled me from behind. Automatically falling on the wounded man, I wrenched my neck and found the menacing stranger. As slender and tall as the upright of a fence and as gray as new iron pot, he brandished a Lugar and ordered me to move. His eyes hurled stones of hatred as black as anthracite. Each one settled in my belly with a bruise. Rościsław dove between us. The fence bar smiled cynically, took aim, and shot the weapon at the bear. I swiped the air, and the bullet described a semi-circle and found a home in the trunk of a white willow. Rising to his hind legs, Rościsław lunged. Within moments the man was a shredded bloody rag strewn like so much garbage in a bryony patch. I touched his neck. He had no pulse.

"Go to Anapel's womb," I counseled his soul. I found a letter in his pocket. "I'll tell your family." Though his ravenous blood had eaten most of the words, a little piece of the address still clung to white. "At least I'll do the best I can." I shoved the letter in my pocket, thought twice and claimed the weapon then thinking again took the bullets as well. I emptied his pockets. His family would want the personal things he'd had with him.

"Who was he?" Having failed to force his body to sit up, Klaus leaned on his elbow, his head lolling on his shoulder.

"Someone's son." I hugged the bear. "Thank you so much, Rościsław. You've lived up to your name. You have truly grown in glory. And you probably saved our lives. Now let me look at you." I examined the bear. He'd escaped without a single wound. Then, looking deeply into Klaus, I was relieved to find that his most serious impairment was a fracture. "We should take him," I tilted my head toward the corpse, "to Matka Lasu's place. Gerda wouldn't do well if we brought a dead Nazi to my house." I turned to Klaus. "On the other hand you should come with me." In truth, but for the fracture he would have been fine with some soap at my teacher's place or mine. And he would have done better if she looked at his leg, but Gerda and Heidi could help me with Klaus. Matka Lasu was alone and would have all she could do just to look after the Nazi. I fastened the dead man's arms and legs around the bear and secured his neck and torso with a vine. "Will you be all right alone?" I pushed the body left and right to be sure that the binding would hold. The bear nuzzled my face and returned to the woods, his burden joggling like a toy tied to a dog.

I made a pouch of Klaus' shirt and filled it with the Nazi's things, tied it to my waist, and nudged it to my back. I held him tight and trained my focus on a wingback chair. We landed at my Woman Ritual.

I was dressed all in red. He was outfitted in white, a glinting wheat wreath on his head, and without a single wound he was more like the Jarilo I had hoped would come into my life. I squinted and thought that maybe with time I could even feel affection for him.

The banquet I had conjured steamed on the red draped table, but we were the only guests. All the Nazi's things were gone. Klaus glanced down at his clothes, up at me, at the table, at the woods, then at the moon. He plucked the wreath from his head and puzzled over it for what felt like a very long time. A lonely owl contributed a desolate tone from a branch somewhere in the beyond.

"Where am I?" His perplexity fed my disenchantment. "Who are you?" I fought the impulse to lie. I wanted to make up a story he'd believe so he wouldn't know how badly I had failed. I told myself that we could start a new life in the past and maybe even fall in love. I came close to convincing myself that I was noble, that all I wanted was to save him from his wounds. But I couldn't take him home. My house had not yet been built.

And there were other practical concerns. If we developed a life in a parallel time we'd have to do it without Heidi or Tranoc or Pan Dąb. I would have to face the war without Matka Lasu. I imagined our trying to build a house without the bears, without the wolves, without the floorboards from the fairies. I wouldn't have a sink or the bed or the chairs or the beautiful gem stones in the hearth. I couldn't take in all the Jews or make the paper for their passports. I couldn't even rescue Gerda Felden! We couldn't do it all alone. We simply had to get back.

"What's the last thing you remember?" I demurred to gather time to figure out a way to return.

"I was in bed. I was annoyed because the moonlight in my eyes was keeping me from falling asleep." And then he smiled. "Of course! This is a dream!" He pinched himself. I'd never known anyone who'd actually pinched himself to be sure that he wasn't in a dream. "No it's not."

"No it's not. I've made a terrible mistake." I bit my nail and then I told him everything. He shrugged. I don't think he completely understood.

"It could be worse." He laid his wheat wreath on the corner of the table. "At least there's food." He eyed the platter of *pilmenyli*, claimed one, and gave another one to me. We ate our pork and cabbage pies while I thought through our dilemma. "You say we're lovers?" Sex gleamed in his stunning blue eyes. I felt seven year old—scared, alone, and ashamed in Herr Schuler's dirty gluttonous hands. Klaus grinned and grabbed for me. I stepped back beyond his reach. My hands flew up to warn him away.

"I said we're probable lovers. But this is not the proper time. When we return you'll have no memory of this. And we have to go back. And I want you to remember." He accepted my half-truth, and without apology ate a fruit filled cookie bar and sat down.

"So what do we do?" He had issued a challenge.

I thought of calling Matka Lasu, but the timing was crucial. She wouldn't know exactly when we had left. And neither would Heidi. I was on my own. I sucked a breath and then another, and, postponing the attempt, I gulped another three breaths into my lungs. "I'm going to fix this," I prayed as I wrapped my arms around him and focused on the elderberry bush.

I was just a little early. The forest crackled and crunched as the bear conveyed his burden through the trees. The wounded Klaus, his blue shirt torn, his eyes all puffy and bruised, one shoe missing, tried to get up from the ground. "Your leg is broken. Don't move." The Nazi's things lay in a heap. "I need to borrow your shirt." Again I helped him take it off, and again I tied a sling around my waist. I filled it with the dead man's things, and then I sat down next to Klaus, wrapped my arms around his waist but changed my mind. Unwilling to trust my own efforts again, I summoned Heidi. Nothing happened. I called on her again.

"Let's make a litter," he suggested.

"I can't pull you by myself, and the jostling would be painful for you. Help is coming. It's all right." She bumped my arm when she appeared. I told her nothing except that his leg was broken. "I'd like Matka Lasu to take a look at that leg." Heidi smiled as if she knew more than she possibly could and cinched the wounded man in her arms. I hugged them both.

"You'll feel a rush and then you'll find yourself in a strange house." She explained. "But everybody there is friendly." He nodded. "Are you ready?" He nodded again. We landed on Matka Lasu's bed. Tranoc, who had been consulting a map, got up to brew a pot of tea. Matka Lasu found the lavender soap.

"Breathe deeply of this," she advised as she washed him. "The scent of lavender can ease all kinds of pain." She tore his pants leg. "Did you find anything besides this break?" I shook my head. "Heidi, get me a few straight twigs." Heidi ran up the stairs. "And stout," she amended. Heidi failed to close the door when she left. "How did this happen? Never mind. Breathe deeply now. Kochanie, hold the soap up to his nose." She set his leg with a twitch. He blanched. "Put your head down." She nudged his head between his knees.

"This tea will help the pain." Tranoc gave him a cup. "It's white willow, mint, and meadowsweet." The man drank. I fetched the binding. Matka Lasu fetched her scissors and cut the pant leg off above the knee.

"Now how did this happen?" Matka Lasu asked again as Heidi ran down the steps. Again the question went unanswered.

"Rościsław is outside, and he has a dead soldier strapped to him." She gave the twigs to my teacher.

"The dead can wait. Right now we're very busy with the living. Now tell me how this happened."

"The soldier hit me with his car." My teacher knotted the twigs in place.

"An accident?" I wrapped his lower leg with white binding.

"Oh no. He veered to do it. And when I ran into the field and he got out and pursued me on foot. That's when he broke my leg. He would have broken the other but the bear scared him into the woods."

"What were you doing there?" I tied the swaddling in place.

"I was going to see Elsa Baumann." Fear froze my blood to slush. I forced my tone to stay flat.

"What for?" I tucked my trembling hands beneath my thighs and focused so narrowly on the wounded man that I couldn't see anything but his face, could hear nothing except his voice.

"I'm in the underground. I bring fleeing people to her." My heart floundered to punch the icy blood through my veins.

"The Nazis know?"

"I don't think so. But they know I'm a Jew."

"Refuse to think that!" Tranoc's bark snapped in two the premonition of my mother being carted away. Startled, I jumped and nearly fell into Klaus. "You attract what you imagine. See her doing her work." His voice, having softened, wrapped around me like a kiss. He laid his hand on my crown then rubbed a circle on my back. "Now let's do what we can for that soldier."

I dumped the dead man's belongings on the kitchen table. "Be gentle, Kochanie. He was once a living man." My teacher pulled the lamp closer and examined the letter. "Could you get me a candle, Kochanie?" I brought two. She nudged them closer to the lamp and squinted. I fetched two more and placed them next to the others. "I think it's Neuburg! Is that far?" I shrugged and looked to Heidi.

"Very far," the child sighed.

"I see s-t-r-something-something-s-e." She tapped the table with each letter she pronounced.

"That's *strasse*. That's only the German word for street," Heidi noted. "What comes before that?" She sighed again. "I really should get back to Gerda. She was napping. She'll be afraid if she awakens alone."

"I'm not sure." Matka Lasu, ignoring the comment, merely responded to the question. "He really bled! Rościsław sure made a mess!"

"Rościsław saved our lives," I defended.

"I know he did, Kochanie." She knuckled her eyes. "I just wish he had been neater about it." Her smile was tired. "I'll see more clearly in a trance." She closed her eyes and in a heartbeat gently swayed. She held the envelope up to her forehead and moaned. "Oh there's pain in that house." She was silent for a while. Klaus coughed. I touched his chest to quiet him. Heidi sat on the green chair. Tranoc perched on the stool and leaned toward Matka Lasu as if to boost her concentration. "Adolph-Hitler-Strasse," she groaned. "I don't believe that! Yes! It's Adolph-Hitler-Strasse! I see the house. A woman weeps. She hugs a child. It's a boy. He's five years old. She knows her husband is dead." Ignoring Klaus, I tiptoed over and sat on Tranoc's lap. I too tilted toward my teacher. "I've lost her. She's in Neuburg, 14 Adolph-Hitler-Strasse." Her words were such a staccato and her German was so Polish I had to strain my ears to understand. She rubbed her eyes again and yawned. I wrote the address, not altogether sure I had it right. "Now at least we know where we can send his things. But what do we do with him?"

"I can take him," Heidi peeped from the broken green chair. "If Judy can be there for Gerda."

"I'll go with you," Tranoc offered. "And I'll pack up his things."

"I'll close his wounds and wash the body. Kochanie, come with me. You and Heidi can clean up his clothes."

We gathered sage soap and cloths and a towel and a sheet and hurried up the stairs. Rościsław was gone. The soldier lay on the ground. We laid the drop sheet and rolled him onto it. "Help me to undress him." My teacher knelt by the man. Heidi and I knelt down too. I unbuttoned the shreds that remained of his tunic and laid them next to Heidi's knee. Wrestling with the body we removed his other clothes one bloody tattered piece at a time. His arms were torn to the tendons. His face was peeled away from muscle. Two ribs poked through his blood-rusted skin.

My teacher spoke to the wounds. I could not hear her words. Then she drew a pail of water and washed her hands with the sage soap. She soaked a cloth in clear liquid and daubed it to his face. "You're not using soap?"

"His wife will want his scent. I'll preserve him so she gets what she needs. Wash your hands near the clothing and then tell it to be clean." She shook her head. "Everything is such a terrible mess. You'll have to touch it all to mend it too." I took the soap she had used and washed my hands as she'd instructed and then focused on creating the spell.

"This uniform is clean, whole, and perfectly pressed. To soothe his wife this soldier must look his very best." I said the words three times while Heidi and I ran our hands the length of the outfit. "As I say it, so it is."

"So it is," Heidi repeated.

"So it is." Matka Lasu took a break from her washing to catch up with sealing the spell. All the blood stains were gone. The pants were pressed and crisply creased. The tunic's buttons were as shiny as the dew.

My teacher touched each laceration and then pressed her palms together, and as she did his skin closed over the wounds. And when she was through, the man looked ready to sit up, to rub the death sleep from his eyes, to wear his uniform again, and to swagger back into the woods. "What will we tell her?" I pulled his boxers to his waist.

"The truth," Tranoc frowned from the door. "That we didn't see what happened. That we found him on the stoop." He twitched his hand. "All right.

So we don't have a stoop. But as lies go it's not a very big one. It's better than saying he was mauled by a bear while trying to murder two people."

"Why was he here?" Heidi posed the single question that no one else had thought to ask.

"I may have an idea." Tranoc showed us a book the size of an oak leaf and as thick as a stone.

"A German-Polish dictionary?" I fumbled through the pages. "And one with such tiny print? Why would he want this?" I gave it to my teacher. She pensively leafed through it too.

"The pages are bloody. So are the other things. And if we clean them the print will vanish too." She dropped the book into the sack with the soldier's other things. "I've been getting bad feelings about Nazis in Poland. We should check the magic bowl about that soon." She added the soldier's beaked cap to the bag. "The only thing that makes sense is to tell her the whole truth. Or hold his things, and I think that would be cruel."

"Either way it would be cruel." Tranoc patted the sack.

"But at least she would know the truth. And I'm sure, blood or not, her husband's things will be precious. Would you rather I went? We have to do it now. The preservation spell will last just a short time."

"It would be better I think. You're much more agile with words. And then I could get back to my map. Heidi could be there for Gerda when she wakes. And Judy," he winked, "could look after her Klaus." She sat down and cradled the Nazi in her arms, hung the sack on her arm, and was gone. "Would you like to see what happens in the magic bowl?" I shook my head. I knew it wouldn't be good.

"Do you want me to help?" If Heidi had a watch she would have consulted it.

"No you go on ahead. We'll put this stuff away. Tell Gerda I'll be home when I can." Tranoc gathered the sheet and the towel and the cloths. I got the soap and drew an extra pail of water. "Are you all right?" I tossed at Klaus as I enveloped the soaps in little cloths and dropped them into their bowls. I placed the bowls in their places on the magic shelves. Tranoc rolled up the laundry then went back to his map.

"I have to pee." The man who'd be my lover scowled at the stairs.

"Oh that's easy," I assured. "Just sit your way up." Extending my leg, I sat on the first step then using my hands pushed myself up tread by tread until I was seated at the top. "From there it gets hard. You'll have to lean on me. Getting down may be difficult too."

He scaled the stairs as I'd shown and at the top got to his foot and bending the splinted leg, leaned on me. "You're lucky that he broke it below the knee. A fractured thigh would be much more awkward." Hopping on one foot and holding me for balance, he made it to a tree about three meters from the house. I turned my head when he unbuttoned his fly.

"I've seen you before," he noted when he'd finished and had buttoned up his fly again. He peered into my face as if he could unravel the strand of my thoughts through my irises.

"I was a child." I nodded. "You brought me some shoes."

"Do you know you have beautiful eyes?" He snapped a sprig from a young pine and tucked it in my hair. "They're like April grass after a rain."

"So you're a poet?" I wasn't sure I trusted him.

"No, just a lowly clerk. But I read a great deal. 'All theory, dear friend, is gray, but the golden tree of actual life springs ever green.' Johann Wolfgang von Goethe wrote that. And until I saw your eyes I didn't feel in my heart the truth and the beauty of the line. All life sparkles from your eyes."

"My eyes change colors," I blundered. I studied a fern so I wouldn't have to look at him. "We should get back." I needed to talk to my teacher about Mama but also about Klaus. I descended the stairs backward holding up his broken leg while he sat his way to the bottom step. "Here. Sit in the wingback." I pulled up a kitchen chair and fluffed a pillow on it then placed his bad leg on the homemade ottoman. "You want to keep this elevated, but it's nice by the hearth. Much nicer than over on the bed." I added a log though the fire was fine. "Are you hungry?" He shook his head. "Tranoc? Are you hungry?" He grunted. I didn't know if I should take that as an answer. I shrugged and sank into the other easy chair and gazed into the orange-yellow flames. "Matka Lasu calls the fire her winter bouquet, though she has a fire every day."

"Is that right?" He laid his head back. "You have a pretty name." He propped the good leg up next to the splinted one. "Kochanie. I've never heard of it before."

"Oh that's not my name. That's what Matka Lasu calls me. It's an endearment like *liebchen*. My name's Judy. My mother named me for character in a book that was making the rounds when she was pregnant. I don't remember its title, but every town woman read it and in the end every farm woman too." The fire called me. I needed to enter the flames to find out what it wanted to tell me.

"What's your last name?" I gritted my teeth.

"Baumann." Frustration sliced a point to my voice that I'd hoped determination would blunt. "I'm Elsa Baumann's daughter." I rounded my tone. The man couldn't know that I was trying to focus on the wisdom within the fire. "She brings the Jews to us, and we make passports for them and then ask them if they'd like to go or stay. And then Tranoc and others take the ones who want to go. In fact there's a run tonight. That's why Tranoc," I nodded to the paper littered table, "is studying the map. They take a different route each time." Crinkling my nose and tilting my head, I gave him a full Felden smile. "I'm feeling kind of tired. I think I'll take a nap. Do you need anything before I do?" He shook his head and settled back and then, sheathed in blessed peace, I cleared my mind then simply waited for the flames.

The fire's fingers had gouged a charcoal cave in the orange. I went in and found my mother on her deathbed. Her eyes were slits in the swirling wrinkles charting her face, and her hair was just tufts of feather white. I knelt beside the bed and stroked her chicken claw hand then kissed it and drew it to my cheek. A flimsy veil I hadn't noticed fluttered shyly by her side, and a misty figure rippled behind it. The curtain parted and a young woman entered the room, smiled, and blew a kiss to me. And I knew the apparition was my grandmother, though I'd never seen her anything but old. I kissed my mother's wrist again and placed her arm by her side. Grand Mama took her other hand, and the moment they touched my mother's brittle body plumped. Her corn-silk hair was softly curled, her face as smooth as a peach. She rose as lithely as a girl and kissed her mother on both cheeks, turned back to me with a smile, and blew a kiss. And then they passed right through the veil and the entire scene was gone. I was seated in the wingback chair again. "She'll be safe," I sighed. I opened my eyes. Matka Lasu tilted toward me from the stool she had pulled from the table to the chair in which I sat. She stroked my hair and smelled the pine. She didn't ask me any questions.

"A gift from Klaus." I tweaked the little sprig of pine from my hair. "My mother's safe. When she dies it will be of old age, and Grand Mama will be with her." I brushed my palm with the twig. "How was it with Frau Nazi?"

"Her name is Maurer, Hilde Maurer. It was hard on her. But she was glad to have his body and things." She gazed into my eyes. "What is it Kochanie?" I glanced over to Tranoc and Klaus. Tranoc was absorbed in drawing out his route. Klaus seemed to have fallen asleep. Nonetheless, I wanted to talk to her in private. I suggested that we go outside.

"The floral taste has gone away," my teacher read my mind. She sat cross legged on the ground and, patting the leaves, invited me to sit next to her. Wishing I were small enough to fit into her lap, I tucked my feet beneath my hips and leaned on her.

"And I don't know that I trust it. All the blessings have been tainted. Gerda Felden's badly damaged, Gerhard Blaustein is in danger, and I don't know that I like Klaus all that well." She gazed into the trees. A cloud rolled over the sun, cutting off the light the sky had poured between the leaves. A sparrow landed by my foot, cheeped once, and flew away. A warbler settled on a branch and preened a bit. My teacher drew a quivering breath.

"War taints everything Kochanie." She propped her elbow on her knee and rested her forehead in her hand. She seemed to shrink. Her complexion even seemed to fade. She looked at me and shook her head. Her eyes, maple brown in more neutral moods, had gone mushroom soil dark with just a few flecks of red. I tried search inside her eyes for the sorrow's source, but the grief that colored them was opaque. She sighed again and bit her lip. I felt petty and small for having burdened her with my disappointments. She squared her shoulders and, with a palpable will, trained her focus exclusively on me. "Gerda's healing, Kochanie." Her eyes were back to brown. "I know her psychic wounds are deep, but she wouldn't even have survived if you hadn't cared so much." She patted my knee and a hint of yellow hope crept around the edges of her eyes. "I'm proud of you for that. You worked hard on her behalf, even if you nearly drove us crazy. And Bożena and the child are going to be fine. So will Gerhard if he does as we've told him."

"But he won't." My voice was flat.

"No he won't," she admitted. "I think he's destined to die in this despicable war. So many people are."

"We're all destined to die." I let the words spill from my mouth with the carelessness of one for whom death was still abstract.

"But not in our youth and not in such a hateful way." She gazed off again then looked up at the sky and curled her hand around her mouth. The cloud had rolled on, and the sunlight was back, but it failed to bring us any joy. "You say you don't like Klaus?"

"No I didn't say that. I just don't love him, and I know I'm supposed to." She squinted, jerked her head back, and tilted her chin.

"Why do you think that? You're free to love whom you choose. But give the poor man a chance." I told her of our landing at my woman ritual and the fear and shame I'd felt at his advances.

"I want my first time to be special. I want it to be right. And I knew he didn't care about that."

"You told him you were lovers?"

"I said we might be." She looked at me askance. "Well that's what I meant to say."

"So he thought it was all right? Don't you understand, Kochanie? He thought you were willing. You have to say what you mean. In any case, these things are much simpler for men. They use their eyes to fall in lust. Love for them can come much later. Women want to be in love. And we have to be wooed, because women use our minds and hearts to fall in love. Give him time. If he's the one you'll know it soon enough. And if he's not," she shrugged, "you'll find somebody else. But there's more." She waited. I admitted the truth.

"I wanted a hero bulging with muscles who could literally sweep me off my feet. I wanted him to come on the back of a white horse all golden and gleaming in the sun. I wanted him so handsome he'd take my breath away and stop my heartbeat when I looked at him. I wanted flowers and music and elegant prose. No! I wanted poetry. I wanted it all. And look what I got." I kicked a stone. "A broken man who can't even take a pee unless somebody's there to help him."

"Yes, he's only a man, a bit broken but good." She patted my knee. "Have you considered that maybe he came to you broken, as you say, is because you're going to have to be partners? You won't be young and healthy for the whole of your life." She raised her eyebrows and tilted her head. "If you want him to be there when you need his help, it's only fair that you should be there for him."

I didn't know it at the time, but of course she was right. I wrote her words in my *lechebnik,* my faithful book of shadows but also tucked them in a pocket of my heart.

Fifty and Counting

Sue Stewart

I've been coming to Tisbury, Massachusetts on Martha's Vineyard for nine years now. At the moment, I'm reclining on an old Adirondack chair that matches the patio set that looks so bad it looks good. In my jammies with an afghan around my shoulders, the mood is deeply mellow. The early morning solemnity is interrupted only when the osprey fly overhead chatting to each other. For each splash on the shore, the waves seem to lap in and out melting away my stress and daily concerns. Being here right now is better than a Valium IV drip.

My other life eleven months of the year is never far from my mind even here in my Shangri-La. My small ad agency in downtown Chicago isn't on the Miracle Mile, but it could certainly be categorized as a significant phenomenon. Being my own boss has been an enjoyable experience. I'm a bit unmanageable. Just ask my previous employers.

My peaceful reverie is disturbed by Stevie's voice and the smell of bacon floating down from the cottage.

"Jefferson, get your ass in here." As Tom Jones would say, she's a lady.

Walking toward the cabin, the sand sticks to my feet. I hate sand. The feel of it on the bottom of my feet and in between my toes is like watching Uncle Ned cleaning his teeth with a dime on Christmas Day. Creepy. Sand or no sand, Tisbury and my little rented cottage are so worth it. Coming here each year is the one thing in my life that is sacrosanct. Death, my own and selected loved ones, is the only excuse for being a no-show. It has everything to do with spending time with people that love me unconditionally. That would be my best friends, Candace and Stevie.

Our friendship started at the Park Ridge, Illinois community pool. I was thirteen. Stevie and Candace were twelve. I was comforting Candace after Bradley Harcourt pushed her down on the concrete, causing a chain reaction that ended up with an orange Dreamcicle up her nose. Bradley didn't even notice as he ran to reach his ultimate destination, the steps to the high dive. Stevie, a stranger to us, observed the heinous crime and took off toward Bradley. She grabbed him as he ascended the ladder and accidentally on purpose pulled down his trunks to reveal his pre-teen shortcomings. He crouched down and pulled up his trunks, which seemed to take hours, as the crowd cheered and vowed to recall the tale (no pun intended) at every high school reunion to infinity. When Stevie came to check on Candace, she had an orange Dreamcicle in her hands. We bonded on the spot.

Now Stevie is a character actress specializing in roles for heavy set women. It's her job to be overweight by at least twenty-five pounds at all times. Can you imagine? Candace is a stay-at-home mom. Her maiden name was McCain. She lived with Candace McCain, alias Candy Cane, until the minister announced the happy couple as Mr. and Mrs. Winston Morris. She was delighted.

ক্ষক্ষক্ষ

Sitting at the butcher block kitchen table working on my granola with skim milk,	Stevie enjoys a full course breakfast that would make Bob Evans say, "check please." Candace is on auto-pilot drinking coffee, hazel nutty something, as she stared out the kitchen window above the sink. She isn't functional yet. Only basic motor skills. We are always quiet in the mornings.

The cake pans that Candace will later use to make my birthday cake are in launch mode on the counter. I'm fifty today, and can't decide if I'm going to give a damn or immediately take to my bed with the vapors. I used to think that turning fifty was just a cliché, and no big deal. Here's the reality. This *is* a big deal.

It started at my physical last year. Joking about needing emergency liposuction, Dr. Welles took me seriously. I walked out with pamphlets on liposuction, tummy tucks, butt lifts, and neighborhood locations that have Botox drive-throughs. To add insult to injury, a few weeks later the doctor sent a report giving the results of my blood and urine tests. Under the results for urine, it said "unremarkable" which begged the question— did I have remarkable urine when I was younger and just not appreciate it?

Then there's death. Suddenly I have to consider the possibility that I'm going to die. Maybe not today, but it's out there. I do believe in heaven where there is never-ending love with no pain or suffering, but how do you actually spend eternity? Here's another question. Everyone talks about being rejoined with their loved ones, but aren't you also going to see people you'd rather not? They aren't all hell material, so those hamsters have a shot. These are disturbing thoughts.

"Hey Abby, snap out of it." Stevie pinched my nose like she has since childhood. Candace, still comatose, shuffled out of the room with her coffee.

"So what are you thinking about, as if I didn't know?"

"Death and dying."

"Just as I thought. You are such a ray of sunshine in the morning." Stevie got up, took her empty plate, and deposited it in the dishwasher. "You done?" It took a second to realize she was talking about my cereal bowl and not my life. "Go for it." I handed Stevie my bowl.

ଷଷଷ

I look at the clock, and it is 3:32 a.m. No more sleep tonight. Grabbing my comforter and moving over to the wicker rocking chair, I stare out the window into the dark. How did I let this happen? Once again, I play the details over and over. It was early morning and hazily I open my eyes to welcome the day. My Snow White, chirping blue bird moment instantly turns to a freak-out as I gaze languishingly to my right. Holy moly! I'm in bed with Oscar who is so young he wouldn't know what to do with a selectric typewriter if it bit him in the ass. Panic takes over my being. I've slept with a man-child named after a hot dog who probably doesn't even know his own signature whistle. Suddenly the urge to hit the powder room becomes my number one priority. Knowing the slightest movement could wake up weiner boy, I shimmy out from under the orange sheets and Chicago Bear bedspread. Oscar is breathing in the REM zone as my feet hit terra firma. Luckily, the bathroom is only a few feet away.

As I start my trek, this is my first chance to look at Oscar's apartment in the daylight. An archaeologist would kill to excavate this one-bedroom dig. Surveying the area, it's obvious the Laundromat is a distant memory. Clothes are everywhere. He probably hasn't worn underwear for days. There are at least ten pairs in various styles and colors stacked, I can only assume, in the underwear corner.

The rickety bookcase next to Mount Skivvy showcases action figures from Teenage Mutant Ninja Turtles to Power Rangers to the complete collection of dinosaurs from the Jurassic Park series. I finally hit the cold bathroom tiles and glanced back toward the bed before closing the door. Oscar is sunny side up, arms across his hairless chest. He's a dead ringer for Tut—the Egyptian boy king. It's not so far off. Oscar does not wear mascara to my knowledge, but it's a sure bet that both he and Tut don't wear underwear on a regular basis.

When I took a gander around Oscar's lavatory, I had to stifle a laugh. Every man's bathroom is predictably the same—regardless of generation. Lid up, crusty towels scattered on the floor, no curtain at the window, and a colony of something disgusting growing in the tub with an option to sublet in the sink. The toilet paper is almost gone. I conserve the plies rather than look in the cabinet under the sink. Putting my clothes on without letting them touch anything—it's time to go. As a fitting finale, Oscar's exponentially reproducing underwear hang from the door knob, this time tidy whities. I grab the knob, open the door, tippy-toe to the exit, and make a quick escape.

ॐॐॐ

Oscar has worked for me as a senior copywriter for almost three years. During his job interview, we got off track from work-related questions and started talking about Broadway musicals. Yes, I said Broadway musicals. We are both fans which isn't unusual for me but downright strange for someone from the millennium generation. We started doing some trivia, who knows the lyrics from XYZ show, and Oscar wins hands down with his word-perfect recitation of Bill's soliloquy from *Carousel*. Now I had to hire him, even if he wrote like a five year-old. He didn't, thank goodness. His creativity and talent made him a top-notch contributor to my company. In all that time, it was strictly business. I assumed he was in his mid-twenties, but didn't really know that either.

Then we closed the Tasty Hot Tater-Tot account. It was a big deal. We got our foot in the door, and it was only a matter of time before the taters turned into marketing strategies for Tasty Hot's line of fruit, veggies, and more. I took the whole office to a trendy downtown bar to celebrate. First, I drank champagne and then moved into the big leagues and ordered the first of many vodka gimlets. Gimmies. My personal Kryptonite. Anything could happen. A few colleagues left early, deciding they would get the story around the water cooler in the morning. The party finally dwindled down to Oscar and me. We started singing the "Jet Song" from *West Side Story*, complete with choreography. The next thing I know, I'm in Oscar's apartment, and my life as a cradle robber begins.

It's getting lighter. With no sleep, I'm going to look like crap on my birthday. It figures.

ৡৡৡ

"Happy Birthday to you ..." Stevie and Candace belted out the last refrain like dirty cowgirls working part time in Miss Kitty's saloon.

"Make a wish Miss Abby girl." Candace's eyes were so wide. Just like a kid's. For some reason, her Princess Barbie party hat didn't look ridiculous. At that moment, she was that girl with the orange Dreamcicle at the Park Ridge pool.

"Oh, she has lots of wishes. The challenge is to pick just one." Stevie, my partner in sarcasm, refused to wear a party hat, but she donned her traveling Marilyn Monroe wig. After dessert and a couple of drinkies, she will break into Happy Birthday—ala J.F.K. As for me, I'm gorgeous. The Elizabeth Arden twins worked on me all afternoon giving me a manicure, pedicure, and a complete facial make-over. Looking like a high-priced hooker with my jaunty queen-for-a-day birthday hat, I'm very pleased.

I took a deep breath to do the candles thing. There aren't fifty candles but enough to make me glad I never smoked. While Candace starts to cut my requested white cake with wedding cake white icing that are at least three thousand calories per bite, Stevie jumps up from the table to get the dessert forks from the dining room buffet.

"Don't keep us in suspense. What did you wish for?" Candace stopped slicing the cake. All eyes were on me.

"I couldn't decide."

"Decide what?'

"Whether I want a girl or a boy."

SYNONYMOUS WITH ECSTASY
(OR, AN APOLOGIA FOR THE THESAURUS)

KATE EVANS

Veronica swirled around in the short blue skirt and told Betty she was "ecstatic" about her new outfit. At ten years old, I held the Archie comic book and examined the word "ecstatic." It looked alien, enticing—as exotic as the black-haired, long-legged Veronica. I tried it out, first with a long "e," then a short "e." I wasn't sure what to do with the "c." Was it a hard or soft "c"? "Es-ta-tic?" I liked the way that sounded. For days I walked around saying "es-ta-tic" under my breath. I don't remember if I looked it up, if I asked my mom, or if I just figured it out in the context of Veronica's exclamation, but at some point I defined the word as "extremely excited." I loved being "es-ta-tic"—it was the feeling of Christmas morning, the first day of school, the first day of summer, or of my mom saying yes, I could go on a camping trip with my best friend. "Look, we're es-ta-tic!"

Somehow, though, I felt that my uses of the word didn't quite match what Veronica had in mind. Her arms were thrown back. Her eyes glistened, as did her blue-black hair. There was something in her face beyond extreme happiness, something that made me hone in on the "static-y" part of "ecstatic." Blue, satiny skirt material swirled around her long legs, and I felt a tingle of static on my skin.

One day at my grandmother's house, I noticed in the hallway a framed photograph of a statue titled The Ecstasy of St. Teresa. I recognized my word, "ecstatic," in "ecstasy." Probably a hard "c." An angel, smiling with closed lips, towered over St. Teresa, fingering her flowing gown, an arrow in his hand hovering over her body. Eyes closed, lips parted, St. Teresa leaned back, ready to succumb to the pain of the golden spear. I felt that electric skin shudder: a confirmation of my sense of the word "ecstatic." Although I couldn't articulate it at age ten, my sense of the term as imbued in desire was confirmed. That confused me. Why would St. Teresa be portrayed as in ecstasy when she was on the verge of being speared? This was years before I knew the word "penetrating"—and years before I knew that in my family's religion, nuns wearing white brides' dresses marry Jesus.

Over the years, the word "ecstatic" has overlapped with, engaged with, the words "exotic" and "erotic" in my mind. I don't recall how and when I learned "exotic" and "erotic," but they feel related to "ecstatic" to me. They all begin with an "e", end with a "c", and have a "t" and an "i" in the middle. They are charged with a similar electric quality. They convey desire. When I read Audre Lorde's treatise on "the erotic," sparks flew off the page. When I read post-colonial theories about "exoticizing" the Other, I had to work hard to resist the pleasures of the word "exotic." Perhaps that was the point of such literature.

※※※

I don't think it's a coincidence that twice in my life I've fallen in love in English classes. More than twice, if you count crushes on teachers. Once I wrote a poem about desire in the classroom; desire that, like Audre Lorde's "erotic," means more than sexuality. It's about the pleasures of the body when language swirls around you like Veronica's blue skirt. The poem is rooted in my memories of my third grade teacher. To teach us the word "palindrome," she wrote "level" on the board and asked us what we noticed about it. As she slid the tip of her ruler beneath the word, she said, "See how it's the same both forward and backward?" It was a revelation for me. Some words were palindromes; they contained a secret: Mom, dad, pop, tot, toot. (My poem contains a secret, too—the word peep, a palindrome.) Afterward, Mrs. Wellston perched on her stool to read us a story, her dress spreading tightly over her thighs.

※※※

I've always loved words, rolling them around in my mouth. The way sound and meanings interweave, overlap, disengage, reengage. The way one word leads you to a world. Like many kids, I was enthralled when I discovered you could say a word over and over until it lost its meaning. It became something else entirely. You could also run words together, create new words, become giddy with wordplay. Bippity boppity boo. Supercalifragilisticexpealidocious. In the car on a summer road trip, my parents sang, mareseedotesanddoeseedotesandlittlelambsydivey, a kiddlediveytoo, wouldn't you? Then they sang in staccato, Mares eat oats. And does eat oats. And little lambs eat ivy. A kid will eat ivy too, wouldn't you? The untangled lyrics made about as much sense to me as the jumbled ones. But I loved watching the backs of my parents' heads sway as they sat in the front seat, singing. My mom's arm stretched across the back of the seat, her long, thin fingers touching my dad's suntanned neck.

There's not much of a leap from mareseedotes to e.e. cummings' goat-footed balloonMan whistling far and wee in the puddle-wonderful, mud-luscious spring. Or to Wallace Stevens' Emperor of Ice Cream whipping concupiscent curds in kitchen cups. I always associate "concupiscence" with Stevens, since I first encountered that word in his poem "The Emperor of Ice Cream." And just today I came across "concupiscence" listed under "desire" in J.I. Rodale's The Synonym Finder. When I was working on page two of this piece and had a sense of where it was going, I looked up both "desire" and "abundance" in Rodale, writing down some of the words that jumped out at me: longing, yearning, hunger, thirst, relish, appetite, prayer (ah, religious ecstasy), lust, concupiscence, eroticism, sexuality, cornucopia, exuberance, plethora, profusion, teeming.

As I wrote down these words, memories and associations leapt out: The memory of learning "concupiscence" in an undergraduate poetry class. The memory of my fifth grade teacher teaching us "cornucopia" in the fall when as a class we made a horn-of-plenty. To this day when I think of "cornucopia" I see red- and blue-kernelled corncobs spilling out of the horn of plenty, the "corn" in "cornucopia." Words tangle in me, surfacing memories, allusions, sounds, connotations. Words put me in motion. They're not static, unless you're talking about the static in "ec-static."

That's why I love Rodale's Synonym Finder. It's wave upon wave of words. All I have to do is flip it open to somewhere in its 1,361 pages of more than 1,500,000 words, and I'm swimming in possibility. Sometimes I go to the book first, just to slosh around in words, to get a bit drunk with them. I'm like a bee in spring, drifting from flower to flower. Ideas cling to me like pollen, and something blooms. Usually, though, it's the other way around. An image or line or idea has whetted my appetite, and I begin to write. If I'm lucky, words pour out, a rush of energy, a fire in my body. When the fire dies down, I turn to Rodale for a spark. I list out words like stacking kindling. Who knows if they'll make it into the piece. Sometimes they do, sometimes they don't.

Some of my poems are more influenced by the thesaurus than others. I don't mean I necessarily found most of the words there—because oddly, in retrospect, I sometimes can't remember which words were pulled from Archie, or my elementary school classroom, or Audre Lorde, or Rodale. What I mean by a thesaurus-like poem is one that uses words as a kind of list that builds and builds. Kind of like opening to a page of Rodale. Such a poem is "Handel's Largo," which I began to compose in my head while I played Largo over and over on the piano:

Handel's Largo

As though an infant
drops to a tapestry pillow
in the smallest, aromatic house
anchored to the continent's edge
viewed from the fullness of the moon

As though the new moon
moves through viscous space
opaque and hushed
dappled with deliberate,
opalescent molecules

As though molecules fatten,
extravagant and simultaneous,
in everyone's abundant palms
blooming like supernovas

My hope is that through the effusive listing of words, the poem creates an inventory of mystery and beauty, building to a kind of definition of "ecstasy." Perhaps to an experience of ecstasy in words. Or, at least to an image of ecstasy: extravagant molecules fattening in palms evokes a Christ-like ecstasy.

Some claim the thesaurus is responsible for sloppy writing, sloppy thinking. But for me, Rodale's Synonym Finder is like my libido, my psyche, between book covers. Open it up and a sea of feelings and memories pours forth, prompting me to write. Or at least, to remember.

THE JOURNEY

BRENDA HILL

Early Spring

When my neighbor's husband suddenly died, I rushed to their home. Perhaps there was something I could do, if only to give her a hug. Her grown sons gathered to give her comfort and support, and for the next several days her house was busy with friends, neighbors and other family members. When my husband of thirty years divorced me two months later, no one comforted me.

I realize divorce is an awkward situation, but I was suffering from shock, from intense grief as well as any widow. I was losing my husband, my marriage, my home and my security. My husband immediately wanted to sell our home and reminded me I should be grateful he was going to stay to pay the bills until the sale, which, after talking to the realtor, he guessed two months.

I had two months to make a new life. What was I to do?

My only child lived on the coast, and, since I had no relatives in the Midwest, I made arrangements to visit my son to look for a job and an apartment there. In the meantime, my husband liquidated our savings and investments to give to me. I was grateful as I hadn't worked outside the home in many years.

After a week with my son, I returned home - or I should say I returned to the house; I no longer had a home. My husband insisted on filing for divorce. I agreed to everything; my yelling at him once too often had caused the hatred, so I was careful not to make waves.

It didn't help; he wouldn't change his mind. I understood why.

My husband wanted me happy, but I was isolated in despair. Our marriage had been crumbling and I couldn't make him hear me, couldn't make him see. Over time, what he once thought was special in me disappeared in a void of nothingness. I became nothing.

My mother's illness progressed, and as an only child I became her caretaker. Day after day, month after month, I watched helplessly as she struggled to breathe. I wanted to breathe for her. Breathe, Mom, please breathe. Then came the day when she breathed no more, and sobbing, I held her hand as her life force made its way to the heavens. My father died shortly after.

My husband was suffering from his own loss; his mother, aunt, and sister-in-law all died in that short period of time.

I think we were both wandering through a haze of grief. But he still wanted rid of me.

Meanwhile, the two-month clock was ticking. The stranger I had loved for most of my adult life suggested I look for an apartment on the coast. He even offered to move my belongings for me if I'd just go.

I packed the car for my solitary journey.

I had wanted to move from the Midwest for a long time, to be closer to my son and see my grandchildren more often. But when I backed my car out of the driveway for the last time, I couldn't look back.

Today I sit in my apartment, my son and his family two hours away. I don't call often as I don't want to intrude or be a burden. I go to work, I come home. Every day I drive the choked freeways and breathe of the gray haze that lies over the land like a low-lying storm cloud. I don't talk to people outside of work other than an occasional greeting. From the thin walls of my apartment I hear sounds of families gathering, sounds of laughter.

I am not a part of life.

Two months after I left, my husband moved in with another woman. Four months later, he remarried.

I feel like the living dead.

Winter

My thoughts are foggy; I can't remember anything. I can no longer wear the smiles required for work so they tell me not to return.

Day after day I sit in front of the TV mindlessly staring at the images, eating, eating to numb pain that never leaves. I don't answer the phone; I don't want anyone at the door. It's too much trouble to get out of my robe.

When my eyes close, I wake in a panic - what am I going to do? Late at night I get into the car and drive the freeways, back streets, desperate for something, but I avoid people. One night I stopped at the grocers and the clerk smiled at me. Sudden tears formed and flowed down my cheeks.

"What's wrong?" she asked, concerned. I couldn't stop the tears. Embarrassed, I ran out and huddled in my car until I could see to drive.

First of the Next Year

I need help. I called the city council and asked about support groups. "What kind?" she asked. "Death? Divorce?"

"Either, both," I told her, sobbing into the phone. "Please help me."

She called someone and within an hour a woman from a local church stood at my door. I tried to speak, but I could do nothing but cry. Finally, I was able to talk. She sat quietly and listened. And listened more. In tears, I felt so grateful that someone cared enough to listen. It didn't matter I wasn't of her faith. She sat patiently, softly encouraging. I wept until I, too, sat quietly. All of my prejudices disappeared with this wonderful half Apache, half Mexican woman.

Thank you, God, for sending her.

When the holidays came, I was able to spend some time with my son and his family. Seeing my grandchildren was a blessing. What a joy in this sea of blackness.

End of the Year

I'm feeling better. I even found myself humming the other day. I want to get out but I've eaten my way out of my wardrobe. So I try the Personals just to talk to someone, even if it's only on the computer. I don't have a picture as most of my things are still packed from last year. No one answers my hello, so I cancel.

Back to my car and my midnight outings, but now I'm starting to look. I love the lights, all the reds, yellows and green neon lights sparkling in the night. Reminds me of the magical world of fairy tales and guardian angles.

Do I have a guardian angel? I must; I'm still alive.

I even opened the novel I put aside when my mother became so ill. Could I possibly do some work? I struggle with one sentence, then another. I have to get this brain going. After fifteen minutes I'm exhausted and have to rest. I look at the pitiful few lines, but feel good - it's a beginning.

I look around to see what I might do with my life. I have no particular interest in anything, other than talking to people who hurt, who suffer, and I want to help.

Is there anything out there for me?

I raise my face to the night sky, entranced by the moon and all its mystery. I watch as clouds pass behind and over, but she appears again, an iridescent pearl against the endless changing universe.

Can I learn from her? Can I, too, change everything, yet reappear as a precious jewel?

As I watch, my spirit soars and I feel as one with the moon, the twinkling stars, and my creator.

And I trust that I, like the moon, like the universe around me, can find the pearl within my soul.

Later the Next Year

I finished my novel and sent it to several places. One editor recommended my work to two known agents, but one said it wasn't for her and the other said it would take too long to get to it. A small publisher sent a contract, and even though their reputation wasn't the greatest, they would have my book in my hands in a few months. I desperately needed that. I needed to hold the physical verification of my accomplishment. Most of all, I needed the association of other writers through their message board. I signed.

On the boards, I never hint of the isolation I still feel. I chat briefly, but I'm not capable of more. But they're there, a lifeline when I need something or someone.

I'm starting to get good reviews on my book.

It's a strange thing; a tiny spark is growing and I'm beginning to think, to hope, perhaps there is a new life for me after all - if I can just grab hold. I must.

I see it, just beyond my fingertips. I'm reaching...

The End of that Year

I've heard back from an agent about my new manuscript – she wants to handle it, but she'd like me to revise. More upbeat, she said, and more of a happily-ever-after ending. I consider her proposal, but decide not to go along. My story is about a repressed widow in her forties who, after posthumously learning of her husband's betrayal, explores life and learns how to live. I think it's glorious as it's written. I just have to find someone else who agrees. And I have to begin another manuscript.

My funds are running low, and I worry I may have to get a 9-5 job. While that wouldn't be the end of the world, it would be the end of my writing. I don't have a degree in anything, so I'd only make minimum wage, which would barely support me and sap my energy so that I can no longer write.

What should I do?

In spite of my determination to not wallow in the past, to face forward and make my own future, I can't help but feel a twinge of panic - and resentment. After years of caring for others, doing what many women of my generation did, shouldn't my senior years be a time for me to pursue my own dreams without worrying whether I could pay the rent or the light bill? How did I wind up like this?

And if I do search for a job, who would hire me? Looking into a mirror at the gray hairs, the wrinkles, I don't even recognize the old woman looking back at me. Where did I go?

Yet I sometimes feel a little sparkle of that long-ago child who loved the magic of make-believe. Perhaps if I keep trying, I'll find my own magic.

A man smiled at me today, and the look in his eye was the age-old glimmer of a man interested in a woman. Something happened to me - a delicious shiver ran through me and I smiled.

Perhaps I'm not so dead after all. Perhaps I am finding my new life.

Yesterday's Hearts

Marilyn Celeste Morris

I was making out my Valentines cards last week when Malcolm Scott popped into my mind.

I must have been all of eight or nine years old when I received the most treasured gift I had ever had up to that point in my life. I remember that day distinctly; It was one of those brilliant February afternoons, a stark contrast to the frigid morning when we all trudged to school swathed in wool, booted feet kicking at clumps of snow, and by the time school let out, we would joyously abandon our winter gear to race home in our shirt-sleeves. Especially today, we would be forgetful, since it was Valentine's Day and a Big Event in our school life.

Earlier that morning, Teacher (I regret to say I don't recall who my teacher was at that time) had set up on her desk a huge, garishly decorated Box, the purpose of which we were told, was to deposit our Valentines inside. Then we would have our Party that afternoon and distribute said Valentines.

We would all receive a Valentine of course; that was The Rule. Nobody would go away empty-handed even if you loathed the thought of giving your Worst enemy a Valentine, you did it anyway, just to Be Polite.

Some people went all out, and nagged their mothers into going to the dime store and buying red construction paper and white lace doilies and library paste, and they made Special Valentines which were still moist with paste when you received them from The Box; I can still feel the lumps of paste under the red paper.

But that meant the person thought I was Special or he wouldn't have taken the trouble to make me a Special, albeit a Lumpy Valentine.

The Day dragged on and we thought we would never get to the end of it, and when at last our Room Mother arrived with cookies and punch, we breathed a sigh of relief and put away our books. Now. Now was the time for Valentines.

We munched our cookies and sipped our punch, all the time eyeing the Big Box on Teacher's desk, and finally she slipped the top off the box and reached inside.

"All right Class, it's time for Valentines. This one is for..." and she read off the names of each recipient, who, according to The Rules, had to acknowledge the Valentine and thank the sender and then return to his seat.

This went on interminably, as Valentine after Valentine was pulled from the Big Box, and each kid in class had received and given every other kid in class a Valentine, and it was soon to be all over. Until Teacher paused before dismissing us, saying, "Here's a gift inside."

A present? We couldn't imagine. Maybe it was for Teacher. But no. She read the card on the outside.

"It's for Marilyn.'"

I felt my jaw go slack and my knees trembled as I approached the desk and accepted the small box.

"Who is it from?" somebody asked. I shook my head.

No card on the outside. I carefully removed the wrapping, my heart thudding. A gift. On Valentine's Day.

I opened the box. A card lay on a mountain of white cotton. "It's from Malcolm Scott," I heard myself say. There was a slight titter among my classmates. Everybody knew Malcolm "liked" me, although I had never paid too much attention to Malcolm. But all that faded into nothingness as I lifted the cotton padding.

Beneath it lay the most Beautiful Bracelet I had ever seen. It must have been Solid Gold, and it had a least a Hundred Red Hearts hanging on it and it must have cost at Least A Dollar. Overcome, I managed, "Thank you, Malcolm," and out of the corner of my eye I saw him writhe with embarrassment. "You're welcome," he muttered, and I slipped the bracelet on my wrist and accepted the envy of the other girls in the class.

The Red Heart Bracelet turned my arm green and the Red Hearts fell off, one by one, and we moved shortly after the school term ended. The Bracelet was retired to my Ballerina Music Box and it was lost during one of subsequent moves. I mourned its loss for a day or two, and then forgot about it.

Until this week, when I suddenly thought about Malcolm Scott and the Red Heart Bracelet.

Where are you now, Malcolm Scott?

PROMISES

RYAN CALLAWAY

"What were you expecting, Joe?" Kana asked, glaring into the glazed eyes of her husband. "How dare you?!"

"Listen, I..."

"No, you listen," She replied through clenched teeth, trying to keep herself from screaming like she so desperately wanted. "I have trusted you far more than you ever deserved. You've been working at night for years – ever since I met you! I haven't questioned you once. I might have complained that I wished my husband would be home with me at night, but I didn't interfere with your work. I know it's important to you. Most women out there wouldn't bother putting up with that crap. And yet, you cheated on me?!"

Joe wanted to respond, to say something to soothe the turmoil he could see behind his wife's wet eyes. The words he had planned to use quickly scattered into the dark corners of his mind, leaving him without any retort.

Kana bitterly chuckled, and shook her head in disgust. "Do you have any idea how much you mean to me? I knew there was something about you the moment we met. And even though I told myself that I wouldn't get close to anyone after what happened to Chelsea, I let you in. How could you betray me like that?"

"I didn't consider that," Joe said, slowly. "It was selfish, I'll admit it. I don't have any excuses..."

"What is it? Am I not enough for you? Not as attractive as I once was? Am I spending too much time at work? Not giving what you want in bed? WHAT? WHY?!"

Joe weakly stated, "You're as perfect as you've ever been."

"Oh, no you don't!" Kana turned her back to him. She stepped away while holding her head in her hands. She felt like she was going to go crazy if she looked at him any longer. "Don't you dare tell me, 'It's not you, it's me.' I know that's a lie."

"I'm sorry."

"Is this it? Do you want it to be over? Do you want to leave me?" She glanced over her shoulder, hoping that wasn't the case in the midst of her confusion. Their eyes met, and the sorrow in his was unmistakable. He just looked back at her, unable to respond. "Joe! Do you?"

"No."

A tinge of hope briefly touched her heart. She turned away again. Then, something else occurred to her. She paused a moment before asking the pivotal question. "Who is she? Cassie? I should have known better than to let her move in with us."

"It's not Cassie, it's..." He hesitated. "Lie. Just lie," he told himself, but he couldn't.

"Okay?"

"It's Nina."

Hearing the name, one which Joe didn't mention unless he had to, stunned her. He hadn't lied to her once since they'd met, and despite the likelihood of him starting now to cover up the nature of his unfaithfulness, she knew it was the truth. It could've been a prostitute, one of her distant friends, or any Jane Doe whose named he blurted out. In part, she wished he had admitted to an affair behind her back with Cassie. Even Brooke. Anyone but *her*.

"Nina? Nina?! What's she doing here?" Kana asked when her voice finally returned.

"Her aunt opened a business in Minikin Capital a couple of years ago," Joe explained. "She's visited over the years, and recently decided to move here permanently. Nina came with her."

"I'm going to be sick," Kana slumped to her knees on the kitchen floor, literally weighed down by the burden. Her heart felt as if it had stopped pumping and was choking her while he spoke; her stomach churned inside of her. Why Nina, of all people? Why now? How could this have happened? Kana mind repeated these unanswerable questions endlessly. Kana was in such disbelief, that the severity of the transgression hadn't truly sunken in yet. Her instinctive reaction was to wonder if he was playing some sick, elaborate hoax. Unfortunately, the dismay displayed on his face supported his story. This was no hoax.

"Honey, I..." Joe stepped towards her, cautiously.

Now, feeling almost defeated, Kana had more questions that she needed Joe to answer. "How did you meet her in such a big city? Of all the places in the world, her aunt had to move the business to Minikin Capital?"

Joe stopped within arm's length of her and lowered himself to his knees. She heard his every move but didn't bother to look at him. Instead she sat on the floor, looking more child-like and alone than she ever had. Abandoned. Physically she was bigger than the average Japanese woman. Her 125 pounds fit neatly onto five feet and three inches. Compared to her husband, she was almost tiny. Her attitude and toughness usually made up for her size. Now she appeared crushed, and as vulnerable as he had ever seen her.

He had read right through her rough exterior and sensed her pain immediately the first night they'd met. It had seeped out of her wide, almond shaped brown eyes into his. After they committed to each other, he vowed to devote his life to making sure that heartache never reared its ugly head again. He eventually succeeded in helping her come to terms with Chelsea's death. Then he was rewarded with unveiling the joyful, pleasant woman underneath the scars. She had opened up to him wholly. "And now," he thought to himself, "you've broken your promise - ruined it all."

"How did you find her?" She demanded.

"I was delivering papers two weeks ago, and the store had been finished four days before. Her aunt, ordered a subscription. I still had no clue who it was until I walked up towards the store. As I was throwing the paper the door opened and a woman stepped out and said hello. I started to head back to the car when she called my name. I looked at her again and realized that..." He took a deep breath and finished, "It was her."

"Why didn't you tell me? Why am I only hearing about this now? We talk about everything. You could have come to me and said something after that night. We could have dealt with it then before anything else happened and you let it get this far." Kana stopped. She needed to take a breath. The emotions were stifling and overwhelming, but she knew there was one more vital question that needed an answer. "Do you still love her?"

"That doesn't matter to me. You're my wife, Kanako. I love you more..."

"Are you in love with her now, Joe?" She ordered. "Answer me!"

"I can't lie to you."

"So then don't," she said harshly.

"I..." Joe sighed. "I am still... I have feelings for her, yes. But I can deal with them."

"Deal with them by yourself," Kana climbed to her feet. "Leave. Now!"

"No," he fought back.

"I don't want to see you, and I don't want to hear your voice. I don't want you near me, period! I won't be able to control myself if you don't get out of here NOW. Just go."

Joe stared at her, torn between common sense and his desires. Kana mentioned that she wouldn't be able to control herself. They both knew what she was capable of. Sticking around and ignoring her warnings might become dangerous. On the other hand, his heart argued that he had to stay to console her. He didn't know if he could exit the house and leave her like this. Realistically, though, his presence was probably adding to her troubles. For now, obeying her request was the best thing to do – even if it felt wrong. "Okay," He reluctantly backed away, and headed towards the door.

※※※

Kana Miyoshi glanced down at her watch: 10:37. She breathed a heavy, exasperated sigh. The Lieutenant was seven minutes late. All, save for maybe 3 of their dozens of arranged meetings outside of work, followed a similar pattern. Every time, the detective arrived early to greet her boss, only to wait an average of twenty minutes before she was joined by an unapologetic Brooke. Granted, the lieutenant was working in one of the worst cities in the United States. Even in the office she was often too caught up in work to maintain punctuality.

Normally, Kana wasn't this bothered by Brooke's lateness. She'd grown used to waiting, and typically, she'd call Joe or Cassie while the clock ticked on. Today, however, the first wasn't an option. She hadn't spoken to him in two days. He had called and left messages on her house and cell phones, but she never returned the calls. She wasn't ready for that conversation – not yet. As for Cassie, they had talked quite a bit. The single thing weighing on

Kana's mind was omitted from those discussions, however. Cassie, her roommate of several years, had politely declined to listen until she heard both sides of the story. Kana respected that.

She had difficulty applying that same understanding to the Lieutenant's timing. Any employer worth her salt would show up on time to set an example for employees. Especially if that employee was under obvious distress. Kana felt that her situations should have held the highest of priorities.

The diner's glass entrance doors finally opened, accompanied by a brief musical tone. Kana awoke from her thoughts, checked her watch again, and then looked up to see if her wait had ended. She sat alone in the back of the diner inside the booth closest to the street. There were a dozen or so customers eating and talking, spread throughout the rest of the average sized restaurant. That was an unusually high number for any time after 10 p.m. Normally by this time, the majority of Minikin Capital's citizens retreated to the imagined safety of their homes.

A petite waitress greeted the tall blonde woman who had entered just seconds ago. They exchanged polite words before the server shuffled off to survey the rest of her customers. The new entrant shook her head and walked directly towards the rear of the diner. She knew Kana too well. Brooke wore faded blue jeans and a black leather jacket with a patch embroidered into the shoulder identified her as the Lieutenant of the MCPD. Brooke was in her early thirties and although she remained attractive, her age had begun to show. Faint lines had been etched under her eyes, tainting otherwise nearly flawless skin. Several thin gray strands had also snuck into her natural blonde hair.

"Miyoshi," Brooke smiled tiredly, slipping into the booth across from the detective.

"Lieutenant," Kana nodded.

"I already told the waitress I didn't feel like eating tonight," Brooke said, gesturing to the empty table between them. "Cops or not, they might kick us out if someone doesn't order something."

"I'll get a coffee soon. I need one. You already have dinner?"

"There was a really messy suicide cleanup on Chisel Street. It was bad enough to make even my experienced stomach turn. I don't really want to put anything else in there."

"What happened?"

"You must be kidding if you think I'm going to tell you. I may be getting a little older but my memory is still sharp. Remember, a few years ago we were talking about the Jesse Carver case - that 15 story drop out of a window?"

"Yeah, so?"

"I recall some deranged individual who was on the scene making a comment. Do the words, 'I thought someone had dropped a giant panzarotti,' ring a bell?"

Kana laughed.

"From then on, I decided I would never discuss gory details with you again. I haven't eaten one of those since. Used to love panzarottis. Thanks," Brooke said sarcastically.

"Was the suicide on Chisel the same?"

"Thank goodness not," Brooke replied. She paused and took a deep breath. She needed to tell Kana what was really on her mind. "Listen, I think you should take a few days off."

"What?! Are you kidding?"

"No. You almost lost your head earlier, from what I heard. During the interrogation with one of the arson suspects for the hotel fires. You scared just about everyone watching outside the room. Quite frankly, I'm glad I wasn't present. I bet Junior wishes he wasn't."

Kana thought back to the incident that had occurred earlier that day. She wondered if it was really as bad as Brooke had said.

Kana was leaning on the wall beside the door of the interrogation room. Her arms were crossed over her chest and she was staring straight ahead at the wall. The suspect, a tanned man, wearing a blue hooded sweatshirt, sat in front of the round table in the room's center. He was constantly shifting due to the hard wooden chair underneath him. Most of the room had been constructed to remove criminals from their comfort zones. Coupled with tedious cross-examination tactics, it often trapped even the best of liars into making mistakes. "Well?" She asked impatiently.

"I might be more willing to talk if you get me a more comfortable room," The suspect snapped, glaring at the detective. He quickly nodded his head towards the mirror on the other side of the table. "Then maybe you and I could put on a show for the rest of the department watching over there."

"I would say, 'in your dreams', but even that thought disgusts me," Kana remarked. "Besides, you know you wouldn't enjoy yourself unless there was a fire kindled somewhere."

"Enjoy myself? Look lady. That one cop may have caught me watching the last fire in my car, but that doesn't mean anything. How do you know I wasn't just driving by minding my own business when I saw the hotel? The world is full of nosy losers who'll stop to look but won't lift a finger to help. I'm one in a long line of them."

"No, you're worse," Kana sneered at him, wrinkling her nose to exaggerate her repulsion. "I know you chased Shirley out of here with your perverted mouth earlier. It's not going to work with me. Like the rest of the arsonists, I doubt you can even function normally without a fire nearby. You're pathetic."

"What are you talking about?" He asked, but his face portrayed the truth.

"What? You don't think I've worked with your type before? You derive some sick sexual pleasure from watching things burn. And if not, it comes from the flames themselves. It's your porn, and you get addicted to it. To you it becomes better, and more exciting, and you can't live without it. Your choices are between you and God until you make them my problem by torching people's property, and killing civilians in the process."

"Hey, I haven't killed anybody, lady."

"You're too spineless to fess up, that's all, Junior." For the first time, Kana chose to address him by name.

Junior sat silently for a moment. He decided to pour on the charm, hoping that it might distract the cold detective. Perhaps it would even help to lessen the charges against him. "Why are you so tense? You not gettin' any, sweetheart?" He rose from the table with his hands raised, innocently. "You need someone gentle like me to take care of you?"

"How – What?!" Midway through the sentence Kana realized that her ring finger was in view, proudly sporting the diamond ring Joe had placed on it on their wedding day. She frowned and hid her hands behind her back.

"He hurt you, didn't he?" He was inching around the table, coming closer. "Want to talk about it?"

"I..." her voice trailed off.

"You drop these bogus allegations and drop him, too. Any man that would hurt a beautiful girl like you is a loser. I bet you I could make you forget him in one night."

"Really? Prove it." There was a unique tone in Kana's voice that Junior had mistaken for interest.

"I've got something for you," Junior, now within arm's reach, lifted his hands.

"I've got something for you, too."

With the suspect's arms raised, his body was left wide open. Her coy wording had deceived him into thinking that her "something" was the same as his. Kana had slipped her pistol from a pocket in her holster while Junior was distracted. Her feigned attempt to hide her wedding ring was merely preparation for shutting him up. She whipped the gun forward, held it at him, just below the waist and cocked it – just to instill some fear into him.

"He was sexually harassing me. What else is a girl to do?" Kana asked Brooke, now that she was back in the present moment.

"Ha ha," Brooke mocked her. "I love you, Miyoshi, but what you did was totally unnecessary."

"I have your back, you know that," Brooke sighed. After a moment she asked, "What's going on at home, kid? You don't have to tell me, but since you apparently brought your personal life to work today – I'm curious."

"Joe and I haven't talked in a couple of days..."

"What did you do?"

"Huh?"

"Nice as he is it had to be you."

Kana glared at her and said, "Thanks, Brooke."

"I'm kidding," Brooke reached over the table and took her friend's hand. "What happened? Is it that serious?"

"It's very serious. And to be honest, I don't know how much longer we're going to be married. He..."

"Unless you want to tell me, Miyoshi, it's none of my business. I just want you to know that since you met him you've been a lot different. I've always liked you and you've been a hard worker since you joined the force. But, you were a pain to be around sometimes back then. You were stoic, impersonal, and bitter. I've known you for six years now, and it was only in the last two that you really opened up to me. That I got to meet the real you. The exact opposite of who you were in the past."

"And how do you know, Brooke, that the real me isn't the stoic, unemotional person you first met?" Kana asked in a bitter tone. "And Joe just sidetracked me from that? Turning me into something I was never meant to be."

"Call it a hunch – one I've had all along," Brooke answered.

"I hope you're right," Kana sighed.

"I told you that you didn't have to tell me what was happening with Joe unless you wanted to. However, I also said that you've been bringing your home situation to work. I can't afford that risk for the sake of the department. Therefore, as a friend, I am recommending that you put your job and everything else behind you for a little while."

"And as my employer?"

"I'm suspending you for 2 weeks. After that, we'll re-evaluate and see when you can return to the force," Brooke replied. "Until I'm fully satisfied with what I see, you'll remain inactive."

Kana's initial impulse was to argue that she was more than capable of working efficiently in the face of emotional turmoil. She had asked for a one week leave following the death of her former best friend, Chelsea. Five days later, she resumed her job and performed so well that few believed she had suffered a recent tragedy. One remote incident shouldn't be incentive enough to assume she needed time off. Especially considering her solid record throughout the past six years. Despite her logical arguments, Kana decided not to bother.

"As a superior, you're doing what's best for the department," Kana said, rising to her feet. "As a friend – you suck."

"Kana..." Brooke started, but the detective was already on her way towards the exit.

ৰৰৰ

A loud thud startled Cassie, prompting her to jump and stir from her sleep. She peeled open her eyes, hearing three loud identical noises. While the familiar sound was still registering in her head, she sat up and looked around. She was on the couch in the living room of the home she shared with Joe and Kana. A half empty tub of vanilla ice cream lied between her legs. The spoon she'd used earlier had sunk almost completely into the melted, milky substance. "Man, what time is it?" She wondered.

Rubbing her eyes, she searched the room for the clock and gasped upon locating it above the Television. It was almost 10:30. Behind the TV, the darkness outside the window was almost enveloping, even in the house. She had come home in the afternoon to find both of her roommates out, and no messages on the answering machine. Figuring she could do her work later, and exhausted from an endless school day, she decided to watch a movie and take a little nap. That was about 4:30 p.m. "Great! Now I have a ton of homework to finish by 6:00 tomorrow morning," she thought to herself.

Four loud knocks reminded her of what had disturbed her slumber in the first place. She scooped up the ice cream container and tossed it onto the coffee table between the couch and the T.V. To her surprise it landed on the surface without toppling over. Cassie pushed off of the couch and stood, enjoying the feel of the plush carpet under her bare feet. Then she hurried through the living room towards the front door, passing the kitchen on the way.

Once she reached the door, she peeked through the peephole and tentatively placed her fingers on the latch. She'd need to turn on the porch light to be able to tell who it was. Way too dark. Simply opening a front door after the sun had set was forbidden in Minikin Capital. Even living with two people she trusted to protect her, Cassie never took unnecessary risks.

"It's me Cassie," A familiar voice called.

Feeling relief from the familiarity of the voice, she undid the latch and pressed a button on the doorknob to release another lock. Stepping back and pulling the door open in the process, she asked, "Did you hear me walk up to the door or something?"

"You forget that you usually stomp when you walk," Joe remarked, patting her on the head as he moved inside. "Especially just after you wake up."

Cassie hugged him. "I've missed you."

"I've missed you, too... both of you guys," Joe replied, returning the gesture. "What have you been up to?"

"Oh, the usual boring stuff," Cassie turned and walked towards the living room with him in tow. "School and homework."

"I doubt Nursing School is ever boring. You were supposed to be working in the labor and delivery unit this week weren't you? How'd that go?"

"You don't want to know, dude," Cassie shuddered, plopping down on one end of the couch.

"But, I'm telling you anyway. I started yesterday and it was the absolute, most boring day of my life. One of my patients was scheduled to go into labor at any time. Lucky me, it didn't happen during the eight hours I spent there, waiting. The witch had the kid half an hour after I left. Great, right? Then today, I was finally going to be there when the baby came. I asked the doctor who was delivering if I could have a coat and gloves to protect me from the blood. My Nursing School Uniform wasn't cheap. He laughed and said, 'Oh no, you won't need that. Only I will.' What an idiot. Blood spurted all over me as the little guy was coming out. I wanted to smack that doctor!"

"I don't blame you."

"So, how about you? You haven't been home the last few nights. Where are you staying?"

"With uh..."

"Joe!"

"I'm not doing anything, Cassie, and I haven't since I talked to Kana," Joe admitted, stunned by the pain in Cassie's eyes. He had rarely seen the young woman sitting opposite him on the couch anything but cheerful. Cassie had been a loyal companion of Kana's for years. She and Joe had become instant friends when he was dating her roommate. She was his polar opposite. A boisterous 20 year old woman who dressed in fishnets, dark clothing, and matching makeup. He, on the other hand, was quiet and generally reserved. Cassie opened up to him rather quickly. Whether it was her nature, his big, brown eyes, or both, she wasn't sure.

"You have no idea how shocked I was when she told me..." Cassie muttered.

"Do we have to talk about it?"

"Yes, I have patiently kept myself from assuming you're a real jerk so that I would be willing to listen to your side of the story. Even though I've known Kana longer, I still want to be neutral. What you did was wrong, no doubt. But, we've all messed up here and there."

"I don't have any excuses, Cassie..."

"Why did you do it, then? I mean, you and Kana are the happiest couple I know. And you... you're such a straight arrow you barely look at other women. So, this either had to be the most beautiful, enchanting woman in the world – even hotter than Kana – or it was something else. Were you drunk? Tired? Who was she?"

"Her name is Nina," Joe admitted.

Cassie stopped to think for a moment. "I've heard of her before, but Kana didn't tell me exactly who she was."

"It's a long story."

"I don't have time for long stories, but usually when people say that the story really isn't that long."

"Okay," He took in a deep breath and slowly released it seconds later. "You know I spent most of my childhood and early adult life in Japan. While I was there, I was raised by a woman named Michiko and her husband Toshitsugu Mizaki. They ran a few businesses over the years. One of them was that they took care of orphaned children. There were a lot of them at that time due to the American soldiers stationed in the country. I grew up with kids of all nationalities, and one of them was a Brazilian girl: Nina. She was a few years older than me, light skinned with natural blonde hair so... When we got older, we became a couple."

"You guys were a good match?"

"Yeah, we were. We kept each other going after Mr. Mizaki died. And we were best friends. I proposed to her two months before his death, and she said yes. The wedding was set for two months from that time. I went out and built a house with my friends on land I was given by Mr. Mizaki. I was going to surprise her after the wedding with a new house. Then, there was the accident. Two people I cared deeply for died because of me. I couldn't stay in Japan anymore, and especially not in that area. I had been preparing to visit the United States with Nina; and after that, I planned on making it a permanent visit. Michiko forbade us to leave and threatened to never talk to us again. She was great raising us, and I never held that against her. She just didn't want us moving that far away.

"Nina came to me and said she wasn't going to disobey the woman who had cared for her all these years. Not even for me. We argued a bit and at the time, I was still reeling from the accident I caused. I wasn't in the right frame of mind to be making any decisions. That didn't stop me, and I..." Joe lowered his head and swallowed, trying to force down oppressive emotions surging from the memories. "I told her I was going to leave whether she came with me or not. She called me a traitor and insulted me about the accident. That was taking it a little far but, I had said some things I didn't mean also. I just got so angry that I went to the house I had built with my own hands and ripped up her ticket. Then I left for the airport. I recently found out she was looking through my records to see where I had been spending all of my time. That led her to the house where she realized what I had been doing. She also saw her ticket and noticed mine wasn't there. Immediately she ran to the airport, and tried to stop me but by the time she made it there, my plane had taken off."

"Wow!"

"Yeah..." Joe shook his head, and paused. He hated reflecting on those days, as they were easily the worst he'd ever experienced. Losing his adopted father, two other friends, and his fiancé all in the span of two months had nearly killed him.

"That's horrible," Cassie moved closer and placed a comforting hand on his shoulder. "So how... how did you meet her again?"

"She moved here with her Aunt. I met her while I was out delivering papers. She happened to be working late, well after midnight. I tossed the paper up onto the doorstep and I watched the paper land on the WELCOME mat in front of the door, and started to turn away. As I did, the door opened. I was prepared to defend myself, thinking that a robber had noticed me approaching and was on his way out. As you know, new stores, especially those that hadn't opened yet but had items on the shelves, are always a target for thieves.

"I relaxed instantly when a blonde woman emerged from the door. She was roughly 5'4" and probably less than a hundred and twenty five pounds. Her well toned body was complimented even by the gray sweatpants, and baggy white tee-shirt she wore. In this town, though, you can't even take a little woman like her for granted. Her hands were empty, and she didn't appear to have any pockets or bags. Definitely not the thief I expected.

"The woman reached down and scooped up the newspaper, and called out, 'Thanks.'

"'You're welcome. Good night,' I replied and then I turned to head towards my car which was parked across the street.

"'Joe,' the woman said, quietly.

"The way her voice hit my ears nearly stopped my heart. It began pounding harder, and at the same time dizziness swept over me. Wondering what was causing my body to react that way, I turned to face her. She stood on the welcome mat now, clutching the newspaper. Her head was tilted to one side as she stared at me. She looked as confused as I felt. That was when I realized why her voice had stirred me. Only one person had ever said my name in that way before.

"It was Nina."

"Man..." Cassie scratched her head. "That's crazy. But what are you going to do?"

"Nina knows I'm not going to leave my wife," Joe replied. "I love Kana too much. That's why I've been avoiding being with her, even though I'm staying there. I have to figure out a way to make it up to Kana. She won't return my calls and told me in no uncertain terms not to come home until she said. I only approached the door when I saw her car was gone. Where is she?"

"I don't know," Cassie shrugged. "She had to have been here earlier. She was supposed to leave work at 8 and I had to the TV on when I fell asleep. I'm assuming she turned it off but... I have no idea where she is now."

"I hope she's alright," Joe quietly prayed.

"I really want you and Kana to work through it. Please try your best. If you want to stay here until she gets home, I won't let her touch you. I know she can kick my butt, too, but she won't."

"She told me to stay away," he objected.

"No, you guys need to work it out. Are you prepared to let Nina go, completely? Maybe it's *you* that needs more time."

He said nothing.

ঝঝঝ

Kana stood three feet from Nina inside the doorway of Hobby Time. The women watched each other, and had remained in a quiet standoff for the last 45 seconds. Neither one budged, nor did their eyes waver. Initially, they stared with caution, unsure of what the other woman had in mind. 30 seconds later the tension relaxed, slightly. Neither had ever seen the other before, but when their eyes met after the detective stepped inside the store — they instantly knew.

It was interesting that despite Kana's Japanese heritage, and Nina's Brazilian roots, their appearances weren't all that different. The detective was about an inch shorter, but they were about the same weight. Both had brown almond shaped eyes, although Nina's were darker and more slanted. Her face was slightly thinner, and her hair a few inches longer than Kana's.

"Nice to meet you, Kanako," Nina graciously leaned forward, bowing. Her hair fell into her face as she lingered to demonstrate her respect.

"Hello Nina," Kana nodded, slowly, as Nina rose up.

"I was about to close the store. I'm glad you came when you did."

"Did you think you'd ever meet me?"

"Yes. Would you like some coffee?" Nina asked, turning to the counter where a coffee machine was set up. One cup sat on the counter beside it and a fresh stack was piled on the other side. A black case next to the cups contained packets of sugar and artificial sweetener. Miniature caps filled with half and half were also mixed in. "I've been working long hours here to help my Aunt, so I'm surviving on this stuff. I know it's bad for you, but..."

"And you're offering it to me, anyway."

"I'm sorry, I didn't mean to..."

"No, no! I'm kidding! I'd like a cup – seven sweeteners, please." Kana grinned, eyes roaming the spacious store. The glass shelves and table displays were decorated with assorted items, arts and crafts, cards, toys, and antiques. Everything was neatly ordered and the aisles were bigger than usual for this type of shop. Hopefully the tidy appearance would continue when business picked up. "Nice store," Kana commented.

"Thanks," Nina had finished making a cup and carried it to her guest who carefully accepted it.

"I'm surprised you wanted that many sweeteners. In Japan, it seemed the customers used as few as possible."

"Well..." Kana trailed off to sip at the cup's steaming contents. "Not bad."

"You are Japanese?" Nina asked.

"Half. My father was Korean so I was raised in *that* culture more. I was hated by both the Korean and Japanese kids in school, as you probably know..."

"The two don't normally get along," Nina nodded.

"Right. As for the sweetener," Kana said, quickly changing the subject. "When Joe and I first went out for coffee, he laughed for an hour when I only used 2 or 3 packets. Such a pain..."

Nina laughed.

"He very rarely showed any humor, but he couldn't stop laughing at how nasty my coffee was. I knew better than to skimp on after that."

"He had a great sense of humor before... the accident," Nina said pensively.

"It was on its way back," Kana frowned, wondering if his broken relationship with Nina was only one of several scars he'd received in Japan. "Nina..."

"Kanako," Nina interrupted. "I wasn't thinking straight and I'm still not. I am deeply sorry for causing Joe to do what he did. It was my fault." Nina paused for a moment, fighting back the tears. "Joe is very fond of you. He had nothing negative to say about you or the relationship. It sounded to me that you two have even more together than we did.

You are certainly just as beautiful as he described you..."

"I need to know - did he tell you he was married before you did anything?"

Nina closed her eyes and turned her head to the side. She was sure the guilt would have seeped out of her eyes had she held Kana's gaze a moment more. Her voice quivered as she confessed, "I brought him back to my apartment to have a drink. While he was drinking I noticed the ring on his finger and asked him what it was. He didn't try to hide the truth from me. I was so angry when I heard that he had moved on, that I pushed for something to which I had no right. I think the emotions got the best of both of us," Nina told Kana. "We had so much together in the past, and... it's hard to let go of someone like him."

"I understand," Kana nodded.

"I can leave," Nina said, beginning to cry again. She hid her face in one hand and turned her back to Joe's wife. "If you promise to help make sure that my aunt's business succeeds, I'll go back to Japan. I'll have some relief knowing that he's happy with a woman like you. You're so much better than me."

"You would leave?"

"I..." Nina reached into her pants pocket and withdrew a ticket which she held up in Kana's view, eliciting a gasp. "I didn't tell him because I don't want to hurt him. The last time we talked he was very clear that he couldn't be with me again. He wanted to stay friends and have me nearby, but only if you allowed it. I can't promise the same thing, though. So out of respect for you, I bought a ticket to leave in two days. If he doesn't know, he won't try to stop me. I know this won't make up for what I did to you, but it's the best I can offer. As much as I love Joe, I can't interfere in your marriage."

"Nina," Kana snatched the ticket and held it between the index finger and thumb of each hand. Watching Nina the entire time, she proceeded to rip it in half. Then into smaller pieces.

"What... what are you doing?"

"You're not going anywhere in two days," Kana smiled, as bewildered by her behavior as Nina was. "To be honest, I expected you to try to fight me. I was ready for a fight, but not for you to completely turn me inside out. I see why Joe loved - loves you. And I know your intentions weren't to do something hurtful, although you did." She took Nina's left hand in hers and positioned it right side up. That brought the beautiful three-diamond ring on her ring finger into the light. The cut diamond in the middle was a quarter larger than the two bordering it on the sides. Four platinum prongs secured the diamonds in the corners, sweeping gracefully up from the ring itself. "Is it the one he proposed to you with?"

"Yes, it is – was - our engagement ring."

"It seems he broke his promises to both of us," Kana tightened her grip on Nina's hand. "But, that's okay. Let's leave this crap in the past, okay?"

Nina was dumbstruck. "I don't know what to say..."

Kana held her arms wide open and drew Nina into an embrace.

ই ই ই

"How's everything look?" Kana asked, walking over to the kitchen table with bowls in each hand.

"I'm so happy that you forgave me. I cannot thank you enough," Joe replied.

Kana set the bowls of food in the center of the table where they joined plates loaded with salad, fried rice, fish, and noodles.

"This..." Joe observed the dishes, carefully. "This is what you cooked the first night you had me over for dinner. At your other apartment. I never ate so good in my life."

"I wanted you to know that this is a fresh start for us," Kana cradled his head in her arms. "I love you, honey."

"I love you, too," He hugged her waist. "I'll never hurt you again."

"You probably will, but marriage vows are for forever. Mistakes happen. The time to move forward is now."

"Is Cassie coming tonight?" Joe noticed the third empty plate on the other side of his. The chair there also ominously screamed that someone was missing.

"No," Kana replied mysteriously.

The front door opened and the two exchanged looks. Joe was confused but Kana merely grinned and then turned to the door. He followed her eyes to see Nina stepping inside, carrying suitcases in both hands. She glanced nervously between the couple for a moment, and then said, "Dinner looks great!"

LONELY SOUL
CHAPTER 19

MARY QUAST

Lauren woke to a soft knock on her door. It was probably Mora coming to take Daisy for a walk in the park for her. While Lauren was under the weather, her friend offered to take Daisy for a couple of walks a day. For that she was grateful. She rubbed her eyes as she opened the door, not expecting to see a tall, handsome man with a mischievous grin standing in her doorway holding his dog on a leash.

"Hey, beautiful." His eyes sparkled. "Did you miss me?"

"Oh, my God! What are you doing here?" Lauren became conscious of her appearance. "I look awful."

Mike pushed the door farther open and entered her apartment. Daisy bounded toward her friend. Lauren tried to smooth her frizzy hair down and picked up a few tissues littering the floor. She hadn't showered since the day before and she had spent all day on the couch surfing channels instead of sleeping. Her T-shirt and pajama bottoms were wrinkled; her eyes burned and her chest hurt.

"I've come to take Daisy for a walk with us." He found her leash and hooked it onto the collar. "I think she knows me well enough to mind for me. A good jaunt in the park will do both girls good."

Lauren found it endearing the way he spoke about their pets. He was a man with a big heart.

"Mora's been taking her out but nothing like what she's used to. I think my poor dog is getting a little cabin fever."

"How about her mistress?" Mike raised an eyebrow.

"I'm gross," she moaned.

"Here." He handed her a plastic bag with a couple of tea bags inside. "Make yourself a cup; let it steep for at least five minutes and don't add any sugar. Take a nap and you'll feel better."

"Yes, doctor."

Mike let the leashes in his hand drop and stepped close to her. Lauren felt so miserable and embarrassed of her appearance she wouldn't look him in the eye. He gently touched her cheek with his hand until she looked up at him. His smile was full of concern and warmth. Sliding his arms around her, he pulled her close.

Lauren sighed with the comfort of his body. She felt him place a kiss on her head before he stepped away to retrieve the dogs.

"Give me your key," he held out his hand, "just in case you're sleeping I won't disturb you."

Touched by his kindness, Lauren gave him the key and walked into the kitchen to make the tea. Once the water was hot, she opened the little plastic bag. The aroma of lemon-mint filled her nose; her chest began to relax almost immediately. On top of being sick, it was her time of the month and the cramps made it impossible to get comfortable. While the tea was steeping she brushed her hair, pulled it into a ponytail and washed her face. Already, she was beginning to feel better.

Shifting the weight of the packages in his arms Mike knocked on Mora's door. When she answered the door, Tommy stepped behind her.

"Sorry, pal. You didn't need to bring us dinner." He teased. "We're going out."

"Get the most expensive thing on the menu, Mora." Mike scowled. "He makes enough."

"What's up?" Mora elbowed Tommy away from the door.

"Lauren said that you have been taking Daisy out, so I thought I'd let you know that I'm going to keep her at my place for a few days."

"Lauren or the dog?" Tommy smiled.

"Tommy, shut up." Mora rolled her eyes.

"I think Lauren might rest better without Daisy." Mike tried to ignore his friend.

"You are so sweet." She stood on her tiptoes to look in the bag he held. "Flowers and food? What a guy!"

"I'm taking you to dinner and I'll buy flowers on the way." Tommy put his hands on her waist. "Does that make me a great guy too?"

"Only if you buy me chocolate, as well."

"Well, I'll let you two continue your evening," He backed away. "I just wanted you to know, Mora."

"Thanks, Mike. Take good care of her."

Mike nodded his head, not sure if she meant for him to take care of Lauren or Daisy, and turned his attention to quietly getting into Lauren's apartment. He stepped inside, pushed the door closed with his foot and tossed her key onto the table.

When he dropped his backpack on the floor he heard a cough. Lauren came out of her bedroom with a pillow mark on her face. A part of him, deep inside wanted to wake up to that face every morning and trace the pillow marks away with his finger. He wanted to take care of her and be with her.

"Where's Daisy?" Lauren looked around.

"I took her and Ariel back to my place." Mike sat the grocery sack on the counter and began to unpack the ingredients for the soup he planned to make for her. "She's going to stay at my place until you feel better."

"What? You didn't even ask me! She and I have never been apart! How could you just take my dog without even asking? She's been my only company for the last couple of days and a real comfort to me."

A coughing spell stopped her ranting and when she looked at Mike, her heart dropped. Standing there with a bunch of green onions in his hand, he looked like a little boy who had just been scolded by his mother; his eyes wide open as if he couldn't come up with anything to defend himself.

After he blinked a couple of times, a shadow passed over Mike's face and he looked away from her. Placing the onions on the counter full of food, he reached for a bouquet of flowers.

"I'm sorry." Lauren rubbed her head. "I think I'll take a shower."

"That will make you fell better." Mike looked at her with large but guarded eyes.

"Will you be here when I get out?"

"Do you want me to be?"

"Yes, I do." She managed to give a small smile and he sent one back.

Mike watched her walk into the bathroom and heard the water turn on. He tried to reassure himself that her reaction was because she didn't feel well. He couldn't help but wonder if that was similar to the reaction of others when he basically took control of their lives. Mike knew he had to make some changes with his leadership of the company. If he didn't give his employees more choices he might not be able to keep them.

His mind raced while he found his way around the kitchen, cut fresh vegetables to add to the soup, then cleaned the apartment, the whole time thinking of ways he could improve. He vowed to be more open to employee suggestions and criticism. For the following year he would look into giving them a choice in their health insurance and retirement plans.

Satisfied with his plans, he whistled softly as he set out a couple of bowls and spoons and turned his attention to Lauren. Mike gathered his courage and decided to tell her that he was the dreaded McAlister and hope for the best. Part of him worried that she wouldn't take the news well, but perhaps because they hadn't been intimate yet it would be easier if she wanted to end their friendship. But deep inside he fought the desire to bind her to him in a way she wouldn't want to ever leave.

Pausing for a moment to listen for Lauren, he heard a hairdryer shut off. He located a vase for the flowers and was placing them on the dining table when Lauren came into the room. Her hair was pulled back in a neat braid; her face had a little color in it from the heat of the shower. Dressed in a clean T-shirt and shorts, she walked towards the table.

"Wow, this is nice." Lauren smiled sweetly and Mike lost himself in her eyes.

"If you don't have much of an appetite, I still hope you'll try some of this." He scooped some soup into the bowls. "I picked up some chicken broth from the ladies at the deli and added the veggies myself."

Lauren sat down and leaned over to smell the soup. She closed her eyes as if to concentrate on the aroma. Mike remembered what Sybil said about the heart of smell and found her movement very arousing.

"Hey!" Her eyes opened. "I can smell it! I haven't smelled or tasted anything for days. What's in it?"

"Lot's of onions. They help with sinus problems." He carefully set the pot back on the stove before he sat down.

"Don't onions make you cry?" She looked so cute with the girlish look in her eyes. "They get me every time."

"Not usually," Mike laughed. "It's all in the way you cut them. I'll show you sometime."

"Oh, okay." She smiled. "What else did you put in there, oh master soup maker?"

"There are a few herbs." He dipped a piece of French bread into his bowl. "Including Echinacea, to improve your health."

"Did I just hear you sound like one of those natural healing herbal people?"

"Did that tea I left for you help?"

"How did you know that I drank some?" she squinted at him. "Yes, the tea helped me relax and I snoozed for a while."

"Point made." Mike lifted his spoon in a triumphant gesture. "Now, eat."

"This is really good." Lauren sipped the hot liquid. "Where did you learn to cook?"

"My mom showed both my brother and me how to cook; she believed it would help us be independent. But we had a lot of fun in the kitchen and we'll always remember those days." He noticed Lauren listening intently as she slowly ate. "My brother and I lived together for many years and our friends were always dropping by just before dinner so we always made large amounts of everything. But we did get teased for having frozen pizzas readily available in a pinch."

"Did living with your brother ever interfere with having a private dinner with a lady?"

"No," Mike smirked. "My brother was not the kind of man who brought a lady home; he'd rather spend nights in the clubs. Besides, we were bachelors for so long we had a rhythm down."

"Like you didn't spend nights in the clubs; with your looks I bet you had a lot of women falling over each other."

"I never let them fall; I'm too much of a gentleman." He winked at her.

"Right." She rolled her eyes. "You said your brother is married?"

"Yeah, and they're expecting their first; and I just found out that my sister is also in the family way."

"Well, congratulations on becoming an uncle. Are you excited?"

"Yeah," Mike sighed. "How's my soup going down?"

"Real good, but I'm filling up fast." Lauren yawned. "I feel fat and lazy now."

"Why don't you turn on the television while I clean up?" Mike stood and started clearing the table.

Lauren slowly raised herself, fought a coughing spell then rubbed her head as if she had a headache. She grabbed a box of tissues from the counter and walked over to where he was loading her dishwasher. She looked pale and venerable again.

"Mike," her voice was hoarse from coughing. "I'm so sorry for blowing up at you earlier. I'm feeling miserable and I just took it out on you. I realize you are just trying to help because I'm sure you know how a dog can stick her cold nose in your face when you're trying to sleep."

"That I do!" He laughed. "Ariel wouldn't let me sleep much when I was suffering a pretty bad hangover once."

"I appreciate everything you're doing for me." She reached out and touched his arm. "I just hope you don't get sick, too."

An electric jolt raced up his arm followed by heat. Mike closed the dishwasher and stood in front of her. He tilted his head and smiled.

"Hey, that's what friends are for and if I get sick then you can return the favor. Would you like another cup of tea?"

Lauren shook her head and coughed. Mike watched her take some medicine then led her to the couch. He sat down and placed a pillow on his lap then instructed her to lay with her head on the pillow. Curling up on her side, her shoulder pressed against his thigh. Mike carefully covered her with a throw from the back of the couch.

"Does your head hurt?" He caressed her shoulder.

"Yeah. It hurts to have my eyes open."

Mike wanted to kiss the pain away but instead tenderly rubbed small circles on her temples then down her cheeks. She sighed with contentment and he could feel her body relax. He ran his hand down her arm when he was finished.

"Hmm, that felt good. Thank you."

"I brought my sketchbook with me, do you mind if I work on something?"

"No, not at all. I have a drawing table under a couple of boxes in the corner if you ever need it."

"Thanks, but I think I'll just sit in the chair over there."

Lauren lifted herself up to let Mike stand then settled back into her comfortable position. He placed a kiss on her forehead and she gave a weak smile. After unpacking the items he needed from his backpack he sat in a soft chair opposite of the couch.

Lauren watched him through slits in her eyes.

"Are you going to work on *Ariel's World*?"

"Occasionally I like to draw other things besides my comic strip."

"You better not draw me!"

"Why not? What are you going to do? Chase me around the block and beat me up?"

"Yep." Her eyes closed.

With rapid movements, Mike directed his pencil across his paper to create the image of Lauren resting on her couch. She lay on her side with a hand on the pillow in front of her face; the blanket was arranged carefully across her shoulders. Even though she looked weak, Mike thought she was strong. Other than Elizabeth and Lynn, he knew of no other woman who would have let him see them in such a state. It was against some unwritten rule that men weren't allowed to see beautiful women when they looked their worst. But to him, true beauty wasn't from the make-up or the clothes, it was the person.

Admiring Lauren's self-confidence he could also see an innocence. With her eyes closed, she looked younger and he was pleased to capture that simplicity of her; a part of her was always happy.

"Do you feel any better?"

"Hmm," she smiled groggily with contentment and nodded her head against the pillow, never opening her eyes.

He wanted to be a part of her world; to see her smile every day. He knew what he had to do. Hoping to play on her good mood he took a deep breath.

"Wren?"

"Hmm." She stirred slightly.

"Mike Casey is just my pen name." He paused, his heart thundering in his ears. "Casey is really my middle name." He paused again. "My last name is McAlister."

Lauren was still. She didn't say anything or even move. Mike set his book down and knelt next to her.

"Lauren?" He whispered. "Lauren?"

A soft snore answered him. He shook his head and laughed to himself. For a moment he caressed her face, realizing how much he wanted her in his life. He wanted to take care of her and make her happy. The thought of her not being in his future was frightening. As he watched her sleep, he wondered what he should do next but the only thing he could think of was to keep her close.

"You are my soulmate, Lauren." His lips brushed her forehead. "You just don't know it yet."

Gently he lifted her and carried her to the bedroom. He laid her down on her bed and covered her. She never woke.

Looking around, he hoped that some day he would see this room in the morning light. He caressed her head one more time, placed a kiss on her cheek and quietly crept out.

Ebook Large Print Editions
www.vanillaheartbooksandauthors.com

All Vanilla Heart Publishing Ebooks include cover art, both front and back cover, and are designed and formatted in larger print styles for ease of screen reading and to assist visually challenged readers enjoy great books.

Kindle Reader Editions
Available
On Amazon